"Let's revisit the subject of lust," Dal said, just before his head dipped.

His mouth covered Poppy's to part her full, soft lips and plunder the inside of her hot, sweet mouth. His tongue teased hers, stirring her senses, making her clutch at his arms and whimper against his mouth.

He pressed her closer, shaping her to him. He cupped her bottom, caressing the generous curve and she shuddered and arched against him, her entire body trembling as if he'd set her on fire.

Poppy was a goddess and he could not wait to take her to bed.

She was exactly what he needed. And he would have her. It wasn't a matter of if, but when.

Reluctantly he lifted his head. Her dark eyes were cloudy and her gaze unfocused. She swayed in his arms, off balance.

"We'll marry end of this week," he said tightly, reining in his hunger so that he could attempt to be logical and rational. "I don't know if you want to stay here for a honeymoon, or if you'd want to travel somewhere else."

She blinked up at him, still dazed. "*What?* I'm not marrying you!"

"You are, and you want to. Stop fighting the inevitable."

Her face flushed pink. "I never agreed to marry you, and just because I kissed you doesn't mean we're suddenly a couple."

"We should be. You're a virgin. You want me. You belong to me."

Stolen Brides

Kidnapped for convenience, wedded by desire!

When desert prince Dal's convenient bride is stolen, he needs a replacement wife—immediately. And the solution stands before him. Innocent Poppy has no idea of his intentions, until she's en route to his secret sheikhdom!

Sophie was preparing for a cold marriage of convenience, until she met Renzo Crisanti. One night of passion led to scandalous consequences—and him kidnapping her from the aisle!

These ruthless billionaires will do whatever it takes to get what they want, be it seducing or stealing their brides. But the women they've set their sights on are about to present a highly sensual challenge...

Dal and Poppy's story

Kidnapped for His Royal Duty by Jane Porter

June 2018

Renzo and Sophie's story

The Bride's Baby of Shame by Caitlin Crews

July 2018

Jane Porter

KIDNAPPED FOR HIS
ROYAL DUTY

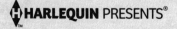

HARLEQUIN PRESENTS®

Recycling programs
for this product may
not exist in your area.

ISBN-13: 978-1-335-41943-9

Kidnapped for His Royal Duty

First North American publication 2018

Copyright © 2018 by Jane Porter

This edition published by arrangement with Harlequin Books S.A.

For questions and comments about the quality of this book, please contact us at CustomerService@Harlequin.com.

Printed in U.S.A.

New York Times and *USA TODAY* bestselling author **Jane Porter** has written forty romances and eleven women's fiction novels since her first sale to Harlequin in 2000. A five-time RITA® Award finalist, Jane is known for her passionate, emotional and sensual novels, and loves nothing more than alpha heroes, exotic locations and happily-ever-afters. Today Jane lives in sunny San Clemente, California, with her surfer husband and three sons. Visit janeporter.com.

Books by Jane Porter

Harlequin Presents

Bought to Carry His Heir
At the Greek Boss's Bidding
A Dark Sicilian Secret
Duty, Desire and the Desert King

Conveniently Wed!

His Merciless Marriage Bargain

The Disgraced Copelands

The Fallen Greek Bride
His Defiant Desert Queen
Her Sinful Secret

A Royal Scandal

Not Fit for a King?
His Majesty's Mistake

Visit the Author Profile page
at Harlequin.com for more titles.

For Kelly Hunter, Carol Marinelli,
Abby Green & Heidi Rice

Thanks for the inspiration and excellent
company last summer! This one is for you!

PROLOGUE

THE BRIDE WAS GONE, hauled from the chapel the way a victorious warrior carried the spoils from war.

Poppy's wide, horrified gaze met Randall Grant's for a split second before swiftly averting, her stomach plummeting. She'd been trembling ever since the doors flew open and the Sicilian stood framed in the arched doorway like an avenging angel.

She gripped her bridesmaid bouquet tighter, even as relief whispered through her. She'd done it. She'd saved Sophie.

But it wasn't just Sophie she'd helped; she'd helped Randall, too. Not that Randall Grant, the Sixth Earl of Langston, would be grateful at the moment, because he was the groom after all, and no man wanted to be humiliated in front of two hundred of England and Europe's most distinguished, their guests having traveled far and wide to Winchester for what the tabloids had been calling the wedding of the year, and would have been the wedding of the year, had the bride not just been unceremoniously hauled away by a Sicilian race car driver. Correction, *former* race car driver.

Poppy doubted that the Earl of Langston would care

about the distinction right now, either, not when he had a church full of guests to deal with. Thank goodness he wasn't a sensitive or emotional man. There would be no tears or signs of distress from him. No, his notorious stiff upper lip would serve him well as he dealt with the fallout.

But she also knew him better than most, and knew that he wasn't the Ice Man people thought. She shot Randall another swift glance, strikingly handsome and still in his morning suit, the collar fitted against his strong, tan throat, accenting the lean, elegant lines of his physique, and the chiseled features of his face. He looked like stone at the present.

Detached. Granite-hard. Immovable.

Poppy swallowed quickly once more, trying to smash the worry and guilt. One day Sophie would thank her. And Randall, too, not that she would ever tell him her part in the disaster. He wasn't just Sophie's groom—*jilted* groom—but her boss of four years, and her secret crush. Although he was a very good boss as employers went, and rather protective of her, if he thought she had something to do with this wedding debacle, he'd fire her. Without hesitation. And that would break *her* heart.

But how could she not write to Renzo?

How could she not send the newspaper clipping? Sophie didn't love Randall. She was marrying him because her family had thought it would be an excellent business deal back before she was even old enough to drive. It wasn't a marriage as much as a merger, and Sophie deserved better.

So while Poppy's conscience needled her, she also remembered how Renzo had shown marauder.

It had been thrilling and impressive—

Well, not for Randall. No, he had to be humiliated. But Sophie… Sophie had just been given a chance at love.

CHAPTER ONE

SHE KNEW SOMETHING.

Dal Grant could see it in Poppy's eyes, the set of her lips and the pinch between her brows.

She'd worked far too long for him not to know that guilty as hell expression, the one she only got when she did something massively wrong and then tried to cover it.

He should have fired her years ago.

She wasn't irreplaceable. She'd never been an outstanding secretary. She was simply good, and rather decent, and she had the tendency to keep him grounded when he wanted to annihilate someone, or something, as he did now.

Most important, he'd trusted her, which had apparently been the absolutely wrong thing to do.

But he couldn't press her for information, not with two hundred guests still filling the pews, whispering giddily while Sophie's father looked gobsmacked and Lady Carmichael-Jones had gone white.

Thank God he didn't have close family here today to witness this disaster, his mother having died when he was a boy, and then his father had passed away five years ago, just before his thirtieth birthday.

Dal drew a slow, deep breath as he turned toward the pews, knowing it was time to dismiss the guests, including Sophie's heartsick family. And then he'd deal with Poppy.

"What did you do?" Randall demanded, cornering Poppy in the tiny antechamber off the chapel altar.

Poppy laced her fingers together uneasily, Randall's words too loud in her head, even as she became aware of his choice of words.

He hadn't asked *what she knew*, but rather, *what did she do*? *Do*, as in an action. *Do*, as in having responsibility.

She glanced over her shoulder, looking for someone who could step in, intervene, but the chapel was empty now, the guests disappearing far more rapidly than one would have imagined; but maybe that was because after Randall announced in a cold, hard voice, "Apologies for wasting your time today, but it appears that the wedding is off," and then he'd smiled an equally cold, hard smile, the guests had practically raced out.

She'd wanted to race out, too, but Randall pointed at her, gesturing for her to stay, and so she had, while he waved off his aunts and uncles and cousins, and then exchanged brief, uncomfortable words with Sophie's parents before shaking each of his groomsmen's hands, sending every single person away. Sending everyone but her.

How she wanted to go, too, and she'd even tried to make a belated escape but he'd caught her as she was inching toward the vestibule exit, trapping her in this little antechamber typically reserved for the clergy.

"What did you do, Poppy?" he repeated more quietly, eyes narrowing, jaw hardening, expression glacial.

Her heart thumped hard. He was tall, much taller then she, and she took an unconscious step backward, her shoulders bumping against the rough bricks. "Nothing," she whispered, aware that she was a dreadful liar. It was one of the things Sophie said she'd always liked best about her, and the very thing that had made Randall Grant, the Earl of Langston, hire her in the first place four years ago when she needed a job. He said he needed someone he could trust. She assured him he could trust her.

"I don't believe you," he answered.

Her heart did another painful thump as her mouth dried.

"Let's try this again. Where is my bride? And what the hell just happened here, and why?"

Poppy's eyes widened. Randall Grant never, ever swore. Randall Grant was the model of discipline, self-control and civility.

At least he'd always been so until now.

"I don't know where she is, and that's the truth." Her voice wavered on the last words and she squirmed, hating that he was looking at her as if she'd turned into a three-headed monster. "I had no idea Renzo would storm the wedding like that."

His dark eyebrow lifted. "Renzo," he repeated quietly, thoughtfully.

She went hot, then cold, understanding her mistake immediately.

She shouldn't have said his name. She shouldn't have said anything.

"Poppy."

She stared at his square chin and bit her lower lip hard. It was that or risk blurting everything, and she couldn't do it; it wouldn't be fair to Sophie.

Instead, she tugged at her snug, low-cut bodice, trying not to panic, which in her case meant dissolving into mindless tears. She actually didn't feel like crying; she just felt trapped, but whenever trapped, Poppy's brain malfunctioned and she'd lose track of her thoughts and go silent, and then those traitorous tears would fill her eyes.

It had happened in school. It had happened during her awful summer camps before Sophie rescued her and invited her home with her for the summer holidays. Poppy had thought she'd outgrown the panic attacks, but all of a sudden her chest constricted and her throat closed and she fought for air. Her incredibly tight, overly fitted bridesmaid gown, the icy-pink shade perfect on women like Sophie with porcelain complexions and gleaming hair, but not on short, frumpy secretaries who needed a pop of color near the face to lift a sallow complexion, suffocated her.

"I think I might faint," she whispered, not quite ready to actually collapse, but close. She needed fresh air, and space…and immediate distance from her furious employer.

Randall's black brow just lifted. "You don't faint. You're just trying to evade giving an honest answer."

"I can't get enough air."

"Then stop babbling and breathe."

"I don't babble—"

"Breathe. Through your nose. Out through your mouth. Again. Inhale. Exhale."

He couldn't be that angry with her if he was trying to keep her calm. She didn't want him angry with her. She was just trying to help. She just wanted the people she loved to be happy. Good people deserved happiness, and both Sophie and Randall were good people, only apparently not that good together. And Poppy wouldn't have sent that note to Renzo about the wedding if Sophie had been happy...

Her eyes prickled and burned as Poppy's gaze dropped from Randall's gold eyes to his chin, which was far too close to his lovely, firm mouth, and then lower, to the sharp points of his crisp, white collar.

She struggled to keep her focus on the elegant knot of his tie as she inhaled and exhaled, trying to be mindful of her breathing, but impossible when Randall was standing so close. He was tall, with a fit, honed frame, and at the moment he was exuding so much heat and crackling energy that she couldn't think straight.

She needed to think of something else or she'd dissolve into another panic attack, and she closed her eyes, trying to pretend she was back in her small, snug flat, wearing something comfortable, her pajamas for example, and curled up in her favorite armchair with a proper cup of tea. The tea would be strong and hot with lots of milk and sugar and she'd dunk a biscuit—

"Better?" he asked after a minute.

She opened her eyes to look right into Randall's. His eyes were the lightest golden-brown, a tawny shade that Poppy had always thought made him look a little exotic, as well as unbearably regal. But standing this close, his golden eyes were rather too animalistic. Specifically a lion, and a lion wasn't good company, not when angry. She suppressed a panicked shiver. "Can we go outside, please?"

"I need a straight answer."

"I've told you—"

"You are on a first-name basis with Crisanti. How do you know him, Poppy?" Randall's voice dropped, hardening.

He hadn't moved, hadn't even lifted a finger, and yet he seemed to grow bigger, larger, more powerful. He was exuding so much heat and light that she felt as if she was standing in front of the sun itself. Poppy dragged in a desperate breath, inhaling his fragrance and the scent of his skin, a clean, masculine scent that always made her skin prickle and her insides do a funny little flip. Her skin prickled now, goose bumps covering her arms, her nape suddenly too sensitive. "*I* don't know him."

His eyes flashed at her. "Then how does Sophie know him?"

Poppy balled her hands, nails biting into her palms. She had to be careful. It wouldn't take much to say the wrong thing. It wasn't that Poppy had a history of being indiscreet, either, but she didn't want to be tricked into revealing details that weren't hers to share, and to be honest, she wasn't even clear about what had happened that night in Monte Carlo five weeks ago. Obviously, something had happened. Sophie didn't return home on the last night of the trip, and when they flew out of Monte Carlo, Sophie left Monaco a different woman.

Maybe most people wouldn't pick up on the change in Sophie, but Poppy wasn't most people. Sophie wasn't just her best friend, but the sister Poppy had never had, and the champion she'd needed as a charity girl at Haskell's School. Sophie had looked out for Poppy from virtually the beginning and finally, after all these years, Poppy had found an opportunity to return the favor, which is why her letter to Renzo Crisanti wasn't about sabotaging a wedding as much as giving Sophie a shot at true happiness.

Dal battled to keep his temper. Poppy was proving to be extremely recalcitrant, which was noteworthy in and of itself, as Poppy Marr could type ninety-five words a minute, find anything buried on his desk or lost in his office, but she didn't tell a lie, or keep a secret, well at all.

And the fact that Poppy was desperately trying to keep a secret told him everything he needed to know.

She was part of this fiasco today. Of course she hadn't orchestrated it—she wasn't that clever—but she knew the whys and hows and that was what he wanted and needed to understand.

"Go collect your things," he said shortly. "We're leaving immediately."

"Go where?" she asked unsteadily.

"Does it matter?"

"I've plans to go on holiday. You gave me the next week off."

"That was when I expected to be on holiday myself, but the honeymoon is off, which means your holiday is canceled, too."

She blinked up at him. She seemed to be struggling to find her voice. "That doesn't seem fair," she finally whispered.

"What doesn't seem fair is that you knew about Crisanti and Sophie and you never said a word to me." He stared down into her wide, anxious eyes, not caring that she looked as if she might truly faint any moment, because her thoughtlessness had jeopardized his future and security. "Collect your things and meet me in front of the house. We're leaving immediately."

Poppy was so grateful to be out of the antechamber and away from Randall that she practically ran through the Langston House entrance and up the huge, sweeping staircase to the suite on the second floor that the bride and attendants had used this morning to prepare for the ceremony.

The other bridesmaids had already collected their things and all that was left was Sophie's purse and set of luggage, the two smart suitcases packed for the honeymoon—and then off to one side, Poppy's small overnight bag.

Poppy eyed Sophie's handsome suitcases, remembering the treasure trove of gorgeous new clothes inside—bikinis and sarongs, skirts, tunics and kaftans by the top designers—for a ten-day honeymoon in the Caribbean. A honeymoon that wasn't going to happen now.

Suddenly, Poppy's legs gave out and she slid into the nearest chair, covering her face with her hands.

She really hoped one day Randall would thank her, but she sensed that wouldn't be for quite a while, but in the meantime, she needed to help Randall pick up the pieces.

She was good at that sort of thing, too.

Well, pretty good, if it had to do with business affairs and paperwork. Poppy excelled at paperwork, and filing things, and then retrieving those things, and making travel arrangements, and then canceling the arrangements.

She spent a huge chunk of every day booking and rebooking meetings, conferences, lunches, dinners, travel.

But Poppy never complained. Randall gave her a purpose. Yes, he'd been Sophie's fiancé all this time, but he was the reason she woke up every day with a smile, eager to get to work. She loved her job. She loved—no, too strong a word, particularly in light of today's fiasco, but she did rather adore—her boss. Randall was incredibly intelligent, and interesting and successful. He was also calm, to the point of being unflappable, and when there was a crisis at work, he was usually the one to calm her down.

She hated humiliating Randall today. It hurt her to have hurt him, but Sophie didn't love Randall. Sophie was only marrying Randall because her family had thought it would be an excellent business deal back before she was even old enough to drive. It wasn't a marriage as much as a merger and Sophie deserved better. And Randall definitely deserved better, too.

"I came to find out what was taking so long," Randall said from the doorway.

His voice was hard and icy-cold. Poppy stiffened and straightened, swiftly wiping away tears. "Sorry. I just need a moment."

"You've had a moment. You've had five minutes of moments."

"I don't think it was that long."

"And I don't think I even know who you are anymore."

She blanched, looking at him where he remained silhouetted in the doorway. "I'm not trying to be difficult."

"But at the same time you're not trying to help. I don't want to be here. I have my entire staff downstairs trying to figure out what to do with the hundreds of gifts and floral arrangements, never mind that monstrosity of a wedding cake in the reception tent."

"Of course. Right." She rose and headed toward Sophie's luggage. "Let me just take these downstairs."

"Those are Sophie's, not yours. She can make her own arrangements for her luggage."

"She's my best friend—"

"I don't care."

"I do, and as her maid of honor—"

"You work for me, not her, and if you wish to continue in my employ, you will get your own bag and follow me. Otherwise—"

"There's no need to threaten me. I was just trying to help."

"Mrs. Holmes manages my house. You manage my business affairs," he answered, referring to his housekeeper.

"I just thought Mrs. Holmes has quite a lot to manage at the moment. She doesn't need another worry."

"Mrs. Holmes is the very model of efficiency. She'll be fine." He crossed the room and pointed to a small, worn overnight case. "Is this one yours?" When he saw her nod, he picked up her case. "Let's go, then. The car is waiting."

Poppy's brow furrowed as she glanced back at Sophie's set of suitcases but there was nothing she could do now, and so she followed Randall down the sweeping staircase and out the front door.

Mrs. Holmes was waiting outside the big brick house for them.

"Not to worry about a thing, sir," she said to Randall, before turning to Poppy and whispering in her ear, "Poor lamb. He must be devastated."

Poppy wouldn't have described Randall as a poor lamb, or all that devastated, but Mrs. Holmes had a very different relationship with Randall Grant than she did. "He'll recover," Poppy answered firmly. "He's been caught off guard, but he'll be fine. I promise."

Randall's black Austin Healey two-seater convertible was parked at the base of the stairs in the huge oval driveway.

He put Poppy's overnight bag in the boot, and then opened the passenger door for her. The car was low to the ground and even though Poppy was short, she felt as if she had to drop into the seat and then smash the pink gown's ballerina-style tulle in around her so that Randall could close the door.

"This is a ridiculous dress to travel in," she muttered.

She'd thought she'd been quiet enough that he wouldn't hear but he did. "You can change on the plane," he said.

"What plane?" she asked.

"My plane."

"But that was for your honeymoon."

"Yes, and it can fly other places than the Caribbean," he said drily, sliding behind the steering wheel and tugging on his tie to loosen it.

"Speaking of which, should I begin canceling your travel arrangements?"

"My travel arrangements?"

She flushed. "Your…honeymoon."

He gave her a look she couldn't decipher. "I may have lost my bride at the altar, but I'm not completely inept. Seeing as I made the reservations, I will cancel them."

Her hands twisted in her lap. "I'm just trying to help."

"I'm sure you are. You are a singularly devoted secretary, always looking out for my best interests."

She sucked in a breath at the biting sarcasm. "I've always done my best for you."

"Does that include today?"

"What does that mean?"

"What do you think it means, Poppy? Or have you suddenly become exceptionally good at playing dumb?"

Dal wanted to throttle Poppy; he really did. She knew far more than she was letting on but she was determined to play her role in whatever scheme she and Sophie had concocted.

He was disgusted, and not just with them, but with himself. He'd always believed himself to be an excellent judge of character, but obviously he was wrong. Sophie and Poppy had both betrayed his trust.

He hated himself for being oblivious and gullible.

He hated that he'd allowed himself to be played the fool.

His father had always warned him not to trust a woman, and he'd always privately rolled his eyes, aware that his father had issues, but perhaps in this instance his father had been right.

Dal's hand tightened on the steering wheel as he drove the short distance from Langston House to the private airport outside Winchester. There was very little traffic and the sky was blue, the weather warm without being hot. Perfect June day for a wedding. This morning everything had seemed perfect, too, until it became the stuff of nightmares.

He gripped the wheel harder, imagining the headlines in tomorrow's papers. How the media loved society and scandal. The headlines were bound to be salacious.

Unlike Sophie, he hated being in the public eye, detesting everything to do with society. In his mind there was nothing worse than English society with its endless fascination of classes and aristocrats, and new versus old money.

He'd spent the past ten years trying to avoid scandal, and it infuriated him to be thrust into the limelight. The attention would be significant, and just thinking about having cameras or microphones thrust in his face made him want to punch something, and he hadn't wanted to fight in years.

Dal had been a fighter growing up, so much so, that he'd nearly lost his place at Cambridge after a particularly nasty brawl. He hadn't started the fight, but he'd ended it, and it hadn't mattered to the deans or his father, that he'd fought to defend his mother's name. To the powers that be, fighting was ungentlemanly, and Dal Grant, the future Earl of Langston, was expected to uphold his legacy, not tarnish it.

The school administrators had accepted his apology and pledge, but his father hadn't been so easily appeased. His father had been upset for weeks after, and then as usual, his anger finally broke, and after the rage came the despair.

As a boy, Dal had dreaded the mood swings. As a young man, he'd found them intolerable. But he couldn't walk away from his father. There was no one else to manage the earl, never mind the earldom, the estates and the income. Dal had to step up; he had to become the dutiful son, and he had, sacrificing his wants for his father's mental stability, going so far to agree to marry the woman his father had picked out for him fifteen years ago.

Thank God his father wasn't alive today. His father wouldn't have handled today's humiliation well. God only knows what he would have done, never mind when. But his father wasn't present, which meant Dal could sort out this impossible situation without his father's ranting.

And he would sort it out.

He knew exactly how he'd sort it out. Dal shot a narrowed glance in Poppy's direction. She was convenient, tenderhearted and malleable, making her the easiest and fastest solution for his problem.

He knew she also had feelings for him, which should simplify the whole matter.

Dal tugged on his tie, loosening it, trying to imagine where they could go.

He needed to take her away, needed someplace private and remote, somewhere that no one would think to look. The Caribbean island he'd booked for the honeymoon was remote and private, but he'd never go there now. But remote was still desirable. Someplace that no one could get near them, or bother them…

Someplace where he could seduce Poppy. It shouldn't take long. Just a few days and she'd acquiesce. But it had to be private, and cut off from the outside world.

Suddenly, Dal saw pink. Not the icy-pink of Poppy's bridesmaid dress, but the warm, sun-kissed pink of the

Mehkar summer palace tucked in the stark red Atlas Mountains... Kasbah Jolie.

He hadn't thought about his mother's desert palace in years and yet suddenly it was all he could see. It was private and remote, the sprawling, rose-tinted villa nestled on a huge, private estate, between sparkling blue-tiled pools and exquisite gardens fragrant with roses and lavender, mint and thyme.

The spectacular estate was a two-hour drive from the nearest airport, and four hours from the capital city of Gila. It took time to reach this hidden gem secreted in the rugged Atlas Mountains, the estate carved from a mountain peak with breathtaking views of mountains, and a dark blue river snaking through the fertile green valley far below.

He hadn't been back since he was an eleven-year-old boy, and he hadn't thought he'd ever want to return, certain it would be too painful, but suddenly he was tempted, seriously tempted, to head east. It was his land, his estate, after all. Where better to seduce his secretary, and make her his bride?

The jet sat fueled and waiting for him at this very moment at the private airfield, complete with a flight crew and approved flight plan. If he wanted to go to Mehkar, the staff would need to file a new flight plan, but that wasn't a huge ordeal.

Once upon a time, Mehkar had been as much his home as England. Once upon a time, he'd preferred Mehkar to anyplace else. The only negative he could think of would be creating false hope in his grandfather. His grandfather had waited patiently all these years for Dal to return, and Dal hated to disappoint his grandfather but Dal wasn't returning for good.

He'd have to send word to his grandfather so the king wouldn't be caught off guard, but this wasn't a homecoming for Dal. It was merely a chance to buy him time while he decided how he'd handle his search for a new bride.

CHAPTER TWO

POPPY CHEWED THE inside of her lip as the sports car approached the airstrip outside Winchester.

She could see the sleek, white jet with the navy and burgundy pinstripes on the tarmac. It was fueled and staffed, waiting for the bride and groom to go to their Caribbean island for an extended honeymoon.

She'd only learned that Randall owned his own plane a few weeks ago, and that he kept the jet in a private hangar at an executive terminal in London. Poppy had been shocked by the discovery, wondering why she hadn't known before. She'd handled a vast array of his business affairs for years. Shouldn't she have known that he owned a plane, as well as kept a dedicated flight crew on payroll?

"We're back to London, then?" she asked Randall as the electric gates opened, giving them admittance to the private airfield.

"Will there be press in London?" he retorted grimly.

"Yes," she answered faintly.

"Then we absolutely won't go there."

His icy disdain made her shiver inwardly. This was a side of him she didn't know. Randall had always been a paragon of control, rarely revealing emotion, and certainly never displaying temper. But he'd been through hell today, she reminded herself, ridiculously loyal, not because she had to be, but because she wanted to be. He was one of the finest men she knew, and it could be argued that she didn't know many men, but that didn't change the fact that he was brilliant and honorable, a man with tremendous integrity. And yes, she had placed him on a pedestal years ago, but that was because he deserved to be there, and just because he was short-tempered today didn't mean she was ready to let him topple off that pedestal. "But won't there be press everywhere?" she asked carefully.

"Not everywhere, no."

"You have a place in mind, then?"

He shot her a look then, rather long and speculative. It made her feel uncomfortably bare, as if he could see through her. "Yes."

Her skin prickled and she gave her arm a quick rub, smoothing away the sudden goose bumps. "Is it far?"

"It's not exactly close."

"You know I don't have my laptop," she added briskly, trying to cover her unease. "It's in London. Perhaps we could stop in London first—"

"No."

She winced.

She knew he saw her expression because his jaw hardened and his eyes blazed, making her feel as if he somehow knew her role in today's disaster, but he couldn't know. Sophie didn't even know, and Sophie was the one hauled away on Renzo's shoulder.

Randall braked next to the plane and turned the engine off. "You can cry if you want, but I don't feel sorry for you, not one little bit."

"I'm not crying," she flashed.

"But knowing you, you will be soon. You're the pro-verbial watering pot, Poppy."

She turned her head away, determined to ignore his insults. She'd take the higher ground today since he couldn't. It couldn't be easy being humiliated in front of hundreds of people—

"I trusted you," he gritted, his voice low and rough. "I trusted you and you've let me down."

Her head snapped around and she looked into his eyes. His fury was palpable, his golden gaze burning into her.

Her heart hammered. Her mouth went dry. "I'm sorry."

"Then tell me the truth so we can clear up the con-fusion of just what the hell happened earlier today."

"Renzo took Sophie."

"I got that part. Witnessed it firsthand. But what I want to know is *why*. Why did he come? Why did Sophie go? Why are they together now when she was supposed to be here with me? You know the story. I think it's only fair that I know it, too."

Poppy's lips parted but she couldn't make a sound.

His narrowed gaze traveled her face before he gave his head a shake. "I appreciate that you're loyal to So-phie. I admire friends that look out for each other. But in this instance, you took the wrong side, Poppy. So-phie was engaged to *me*. Sophie had promised to marry *me*. If you knew she was having a relationship with an-other man, you should have come to me. You should have warned me instead of leaving me out there, stupid and exposed." And then he swung open his door and stepped out, walking from her in long, fast strides as if he couldn't wait to get away from her.

Poppy exhaled in a slow, shuddering breath. He was beyond livid with her. He was also hurt. She'd never meant to wound him. She'd wanted the best for him, too. And beautiful Sophie would have been the best if she'd loved him, but Sophie didn't love him. There had been no love between them, just agreements and money and mergers.

Shaken, Poppy opened her door and stepped out. She needed to fix this, but how? What could she possibly do now to make it better?

She wouldn't argue with him, that was for sure. And she'd let him be angry, because he had a right to be angry, and she'd be even more agreeable and amenable than usual so that he'd know she was sorry, and determined to make amends.

Poppy went around to the back of the car to retrieve her bag, but a young uniformed man approached and said he would be taking care of the luggage and she was to go on board where a flight attendant would help her get settled.

Poppy wasn't surprised by the brisk efficiency. Randall's helicopter was always available and his staff was always the epitome of professional but it still boggled her mind that he had a helicopter *and* a private plane. It had to be a terrible expense maintaining both of these, as well as his fleet of cars. Randall loved cars. It was one of his passions, collecting vintage models as if they were refrigerator magnets.

"What about the car?" she asked him.

"I'm driving it back to Langston House," the young man answered with a quick smile. "Do you have everything?"

"Yes."

"Good. Enjoy your flight."

Poppy boarded the plane self-consciously, pushing back dark tendrils of hair that had come loose from the pins. She felt wildly overdressed and yet exposed at the same time. She wanted a shawl for her bare shoulders and comfy slippers for her feet. But at least she wasn't the only one in formal dress. Randall still wore his morning suit, although he'd loosened his tie and unbuttoned the top button on his crisp, white dress shirt.

A flight attendant emerged from the jet's compact kitchen galley and greeted Poppy with a smile. "Welcome on board," she said. "Any seat."

The flight attendant followed Poppy down the narrow aisle, past a small conference table to a group of four leather armchairs. The seats were wide and they appeared to be the reclining kind with solid armrests and luxuriously soft leather.

She gingerly sat down in the nearest chair and it was very comfortable indeed.

"Something to drink?" the pretty, blonde flight attendant asked. "A glass of champagne? We have a lovely bottle on ice."

"I'm not the bride," Poppy said quickly.

"I know. But the wedding is off so why not enjoy the bubbles?"

"I don't think that's a good idea. I don't want to upset Randall."

"He was the one who suggested it."

Poppy laughed, nervous. "In that case, yes, a small glass might be nice. I'm shaking like a leaf."

"From the sound of things, it's been quite a day. A little fizz should help you relax."

The flight attendant returned to the galley and mo-

ments later Randall and the pilots boarded the plane.
The three men stood in front of the cockpit, still deep
in discussion. The discussion looked serious, too. There
wasn't much smiling on anyone's part, but then, Randall wasn't a man that smiled often. She wouldn't
have described him as grim or stern, either, but rather
quiet and self-contained. The upside was that when he
spoke, people listened to him, but unfortunately, Randall didn't speak often enough, tending to sit back and
listen and let others fill the silence with their voices.
Sophie thought his silence and reserve made him rather
dull, but there were plenty of women who found him
mysterious, asking Poppy in whispers what was the
Earl of Langston *really* like?

Poppy usually answered with a dramatic pause and
then a hushed, *Fascinating*.

Because he was.

He had a brilliant mind and had taken his father's
businesses and investments and parlayed them into
even bigger businesses and more successful investments, and that alone would have been noteworthy, but
Randall did more than just make money. He gave his
time generously, providing leadership on a dozen different boards, as well as volunteered with a half dozen
different charities, including several organizations in
the Middle East. Randall was particularly valuable to
those latter organizations since he could speak a stag-
gering number of languages, including Egyptian, Arabic and Greek.

The Earl of Langston worked hard, very hard.

If one were to criticize him it would be that he
worked too much. Sophie certainly thought so. Poppy
had tried to educate Sophie on Randall's business,

thinking that if Sophie was more interested in Randall's work and life, the couple would have more in common, and would therefore enjoy each other's company more, but Sophie wasn't interested in the boards Randall sat on, or his numerous investments. Her ears had pricked at the charity work, because Sophie had her own favorite charities, but the interest didn't last long, in part because Randall failed to reciprocate. He took Sophie for granted. He didn't try to woo her, or romance her. There were no little weekends away. No special dinners out. It was almost as if they were an old married couple even before they married.

Sophie deserved better. She deserved *more*.

Poppy hoped that Renzo marching down the aisle of Langston Chapel would ultimately be a good thing for Sophie.

But even if it was a good thing, it would be scandalous. It would always be scandalous.

Heartsick, Poppy closed her eyes and found herself wondering about Sophie. Was she okay? Where had Renzo taken her? And what was happening in her world now?

"Guilty conscience, Poppy?"

Randall's deep, husky voice seemed to vibrate all the way through her.

She opened her eyes and straightened quickly, shoulders squaring so that the boned bodice pressed her breasts up.

He was standing over her, which meant she had to tilt her head back to look up at him. He was tall and lean, and his elegant suit should have made him look elegant, too, but instead he struck her as hard and fierce, and more than a little bit savage, which was both strange and awful because until today she would have described Randall Grant as the most decent man she'd ever met. Until today she would have trusted him with her life. Now she wasn't so sure.

"No," she said breathlessly, worried about being alone with him. It wasn't that he'd hurt her, but he struck her as unpredictable, and this new unpredictability made her incredibly anxious.

The flight attendant appeared behind him with the flute of champagne. "For Miss Marr," she said.

Randall took it from her and handed it to Poppy. "We're celebrating, are we?" he said mockingly.

Her pulse jumped as their fingers brushed, the sharp staccato making her breathless and jittery. She glanced from his cool, gold eyes into the golden bubbles fizzing in her flute. "The flight attendant said you were the one that suggested the champagne."

"I was curious to see what you would do."

Her eyes stung. Her throat threatened to seal closed. "Take it back, then," she said, pushing the flute back toward him. "I didn't want it in the first place."

"I wish I could believe you."

The hardness in his voice made her ache. She'd thought she'd done the right thing by writing to Renzo, but now she wasn't sure. Had she been wrong about Randall and Sophie?

Did Randall actually love her? Had Poppy just inadvertently broken his heart?

It didn't help being this physically close to Randall when her emotions were so unsettled, either. Nor did she know how to read this new Randall Grant. He wasn't anything like the quiet, considerate man she'd worked for, a man who always seemed to know how to handle her.

"You like champagne," he said carelessly, dropping into the seat opposite hers. "Keep it. I have a drink coming, too."

"Yes, but I shouldn't drink, not when working. I don't know what I was thinking."

"You were thinking that you're a bundle of nerves, and a little bit of alcohol sounded like the perfect tonic."

"Maybe. But we don't drink together. I don't think you and I have ever had a drink, just the two of us. If there was wine, or champagne open, it's because Sophie was there and Sophie wanted a glass and we never let her drink alone."

"No, we never did. We both looked after her, didn't we?"

Poppy's throat thickened. "Please don't hate her."

"It's impossible to like her right now."

Poppy stared down into her glass. "Maybe it's better if we don't discuss her."

"Four hours ago she was to be my wife. Now I'm to simply forget her? Just like that?"

She looked up at him, struggling to think of something she could say, but nothing came to her and she just gave him a look that she hoped was properly sympathetic without being pitying.

"I'm shocked and angry, not broken. Save the sympathy for someone who needs it."

"Do you want her back?"

"No."

"I didn't think so."

"Why?"

"Because even if she did decide she'd made a mistake, I don't think you'd forgive and forget. At least not for a long time."

The corner of his mouth curled. "I don't like being played for a fool, no," he said, giving her a long, penetrating look that made her squirm because it seemed to imply that he also thought *she* had played him for a fool. And if that was the case, then spending the next week working together was asking for trouble. He wouldn't be in a proper state of mind.

The flight attendant appeared with a crystal tumbler. "Your whiskey," she said, handing him the glass. "Captain Winter also wanted you to know that the new flight plan has been approved, and we'll be departing in just a few minutes."

"Thank you," Randall said, giving the attendant a warm smile, the kind of smile he used to give Poppy, the kind of smile that had made her put him on a pedestal in the beginning.

And just like that, tears filled her eyes and she had to duck her head so he wouldn't see. Because if she did look at him, he'd see more than she wanted him to see. Randall was startlingly perceptive. He paid attention to people and things, picking up on details others missed.

"I knew it wouldn't be long before you got weepy," he said, extending his long legs, invading her space. "Before this morning, I would have said you are nothing if not predictable, but you surprised me today. You're not at all who I thought you were."

She drew her legs back farther to keep her ankles from touching his, and told herself to bite her tongue, and then bite it again because arguing with him would only make the tension worse.

He gave his glass a shake, letting the amber liquid swirl. "Did you know about Crisanti?"

Poppy continued to bite her tongue, because how could she answer that without incriminating herself? Clearly in this case, the best answer was no answer.

"Poppy."

The flight attendant was closing the door and locking it securely, and the deliberate steps made Poppy want to jump out of her chair and race off the plane. She should go now, while she could do. She needed to escape. She needed to go. She couldn't stay here with Randall—

"My bride was carted off from the church today, and she didn't even make a peep of protest," he continued quietly, almost lazily, even as his intense gaze skewered her. She didn't even have to look at him to know he was staring her down because she could feel it all the way through her.

Poppy swallowed hard. "I think she peeped."

"No, she didn't. And neither did you." He growled the words, temper rising, and she jerked her head up to look at him, and the look he gave her was so savage and dark that Poppy's pulse jumped and her stomach lurched.

"You weren't surprised to see Crisanti marching down the aisle today," he added, lifting a finger to stop her protest. "Enough with the lying. It doesn't become you. You forget, I *know* you. I've worked with you, worked closely with you, and I saw it in your face, saw it in your eyes."

"Saw what?"

"Guilt. But I also saw something else. You were happy to see Crisanti arrive. You were *elated.*"

"I wasn't elated."

"But you weren't devastated."

She placed the flute down on the narrow table next to her. "I'd like to take my vacation time, the time you promised me. I don't think it's a good idea to work together this next week. I think we both need some time, and time apart—"

"No."

"I can take the train back to London."

"No."

"I don't enjoy you like this—"

"Perhaps it's not about you anymore, Poppy. Perhaps it's now about me."

"I don't understand."

"I want to know what happened today. I want to know everything."

His voice was deep and rough and it scratched her senses. She dragged her attention up, her gaze soaking in his face. She knew that face so well, knew his brow and every faint crease at the corner of his eyes. She knew how he'd tighten his jaw when displeased, and how his lips firmed as he concentrated while reading. If he was very angry, his features would go blank and still. If he was relaxed, his lovely mouth would lift—

No. Not lovely.

She shouldn't ever think his mouth was lovely.

Even though she'd vanished, he still belonged to Sophie. He'd always belong to Sophie. They'd been engaged since Sophie was eighteen, with the understanding that they'd be married one day happening even earlier in their lives.

The fact was, Randall and Sophie had been practically matched since birth, an arrangement that suited both families, and the respective family fortunes, and Sophie insisted she was good with it. She'd told Poppy more than once that she hadn't ever expected to marry for love, and wasn't particularly troubled by the lack of romance since she liked Dal, and Dal liked her, and they complemented each other well.

A lump filled her throat because Poppy didn't just like Randall, she truly cared for him. Deeply cared. The kind of feelings that put butterflies in her stomach and made her chest tighten with tenderness. "It's not my place," she choked. "I wasn't your bride!"

"But you were part of today's circus. You took part in the charade."

"It wasn't a charade!"

"Then where is Sophie?"

His question hung there between them, heavy and suffocating, and Dal knew Poppy was miserable; her brown eyes were full of shadows and sorrow, and usually he hated seeing her unhappy. Usually he wanted to lift her when she struggled but not today. Today she deserved to suffer.

He'd trusted her. He'd trusted her even more than Sophie, and he'd planned on spending the rest of his life with Sophie.

Dal shook his head, still trying to grasp it all.

If Sophie had been so unhappy marrying him, why didn't she just break the engagement before it got to this point?

It was not as if he didn't have other options. Women threw themselves at him daily. Women were constantly letting him know that they found him desirable. Beautiful, educated, polished women who made it known that they'd do anything to become his countess, and if marriage was out, then perhaps his mistress?

But he'd been loyal to Sophie, despite their long engagement. Or at least he'd been faithful once the engagement had been made public, which was five and a half years ago. Before the public engagement was the private understanding, an understanding reached between the fathers, the Earl of Langston and Sir Carmichael-Jones. But for five and a half years, he'd held himself in check because Sophie, stunning Sophie Carmichael-Jones, was a virgin, and she'd made it clear that she intended to remain a virgin until her wedding night.

He now seriously doubted that when she'd walked down the aisle today she'd still been a virgin.

Dal swore beneath his breath, counting down the minutes until they reached their cruising altitude so he could escape to the small back cabin, which doubled as a private office and a bedroom.

Once they stopped climbing, he unfastened his seat belt and disappeared into the back cabin, which had a desk, a reclining leather chair and a wall bed. The wall bed could easily be converted when needed, but Dal had never used it as a bedroom. He preferred to work on his flights, not rest.

Closing the door, he removed his jacket, tugged off his tie and unbuttoned his dress shirt. Half-dressed, he opened the large black suitcase that had been stowed in the closet and found a pair of trousers and a light tan linen shirt that would be appropriate for the heat of the Atlas Mountains.

Hard to believe he was heading to Mehkar.

It'd been so long.

No one would think to look for him in his mother's country, either, much less his father's family. Dal's late father had orchestrated the schism, savagely cutting off his mother's family following the fatal car accident twenty-three years ago.

It was on his twenty-first birthday that his past resurrected itself. He'd been out celebrating his birthday with friends and returned worse for the wear to his Cambridge flat to discover a bearded man in kaffiyeh, the traditional long white robes Arab men wore, on his doorstep.

It had been over ten years since he'd last seen his mother's father, but instead of moving forward to greet his grandfather, he stood back, aware that he reeked of alcohol and cigarette smoke, aware, too, of the disapproval in his grandfather's dark eyes.

Randall managed a stiff, awkward bow. "Sheikh bin Mehkar."

"As-Salam-u-Alaikum," his grandfather had answered. *Peace be to you.* He extended his hand, then, to Randall. "No handshake? No hug?"

It was a rebuke. A quiet rebuke, but a reproof nonetheless. Randall stiffened, ashamed, annoyed, uncomfortable, and he put his hand in his grandfather's even as he glanced away, toward the small window at the end of the hall, angry that his mother's father was here now. Where had he been for the past ten years? Where had his grandmother gone and the aunts and uncles and cousins who had filled his childhood?

He'd needed them as a grieving boy. He'd needed them to remind him that his beautiful mother had existed, as by Christmas his father had stripped Langston House of all her photos and mementos, going so far as to even remove the huge oil family portrait only completed the year before, the portrait of a family in happier days—father, mother and sons—from above the sixteenth-century Dutch sideboard in the formal dining room.

Perhaps if Dal hadn't spent a night drinking, perhaps if Dal's phone call with his father the evening before hadn't been so tense and terse, full of duty and obligation, maybe Dal would have remembered the affection his mother had held for her parents, in particular, her father, who had allowed her to leave to marry her handsome, titled, cash-strapped Englishman.

And so instead of being glad to see this lost grandfather, Dal curtly invited his grandfather in. "Would you like tea? I could put the kettle on."

"Only if you shower first."

And Randall Grant, the second-born son who shouldn't have become the heir, the second son who had never flaunted his wealth or position, snapped, "I will have my tea first. Come in, Grandfather, if you wish. But I'm not going to be told what to do, not today, and certainly not by you."

Dark gaze hooded, Sheikh Mansur bin Mehkar looked his oldest living grandson, Randall Michael Talal, up and down, and then turned around and walked away.

Randall stood next to his door, his flat key clenched in his hand, and watched his grandfather head for the steep staircase.

He should go after him.

He should apologize.

He should ask where his grandfather was staying.

He should suggest meeting for dinner.

He should.

He didn't.

It wasn't until the next morning that Randall discovered the envelope half-hidden by the thin doormat. Inside the envelope was a birthday greeting and a packet of papers. For his twenty-first birthday he'd been given Kasbah Jolie, his mother's favorite home, the home that had also been the Mehkar royal family's summer palace for the past three hundred and fifty years.

He wouldn't know for another ten years that along with the summer palace, he'd also been named as the successor to the Mehkar throne.

But both discoveries only hardened his resolve to keep his distance from his mother's family. He didn't want the throne. He didn't want to live in, or rule, Mehkar. He didn't want anything to do with the summer palace, either, a place he still associated far too closely with his beloved mother, a mother he'd lost far too early. It was bad enough that at eleven he'd become Viscount Langston following his older brother's death. Why would he want to be responsible for Mehkar, too?

Poppy glanced up and watched as Dal approached. He'd changed into dark trousers and a light tan linen shirt, the shirt an almost perfect match for his pale gold eyes. He looked handsome, impossibly handsome, but then, he always did. She just never let herself dwell on it, knowing that her attraction was unprofessional and would only lead to complications. Gorgeous, wealthy men like Randall Grant did not like women like her. Why should they when they could have the Sophie Carmichael-Joneses of the world?

"Your turn," Randall said shortly. "And once you

change, please throw that damn dress away. I never want to see it again."

"Where is my bag?"

"In the closet in the back cabin."

Poppy located her worn overnight bag in the closet but when she opened it, she had only her nightgown, travel toiletries, a pair of tennis shoes and her favorite jeans. The jeans and tennis shoes were good, but she couldn't leave the cabin without a shirt.

Poppy sat back on her heels and tried to remember where she'd put the rest of her clothes. Had they gotten caught up in Sophie's things? Or had she left them at the hotel when they checked out this morning?

Suppressing a sigh, she returned to the chairs in the main cabin.

The flight attendant was in the middle of setting up a table for a late lunch, covering the folding table with a fine white cloth before laying out china plates with thick bands of gold, crystal stemware, and real sterling flatware.

"You didn't change," Randall said, spotting her.

"I don't have a blouse or top or…or bra…for that matter."

"You could borrow one of my shirts, and braless is fine. It's just me here. I won't stare."

There was nothing provocative in his words and yet her face and body flooded with heat. "Then yes, thank you. Because I'm ready to get out of this dress, too."

He rose from his seat, stepping around the table, and she followed him back to the cabin. The private cabin was small, and felt even tinier when Randall entered the room with her.

She stepped back so he'd have room to open his suitcase and find a suitable shirt for her.

"What are you wearing on the bottom?" he asked.

"Jeans."

He rifled through his clothes, selecting a white dress shirt with blue pinstripes for her. "This should cover you," he said.

"Thank you."

He nodded, and he turned to leave and she took a step to give him more room but somehow they'd both stepped in the same direction and now he was practically on top of her and he put out a hand to steady her, but his hand went to her waist, not her elbow, and his hand seemed to burn all the way through the thin silk fabric, and she gasped, lips parting, skin heating, her entire body blisteringly warm.

In the close confines of the cabin, she caught a lingering whiff of the cologne he'd put on this morning and it was rich and spicy and she wanted to step closer to him and bury her face in his chest, and breathe him in more deeply.

He smelled so good, and when he touched her, he felt so good, and it was frightening how fast she was losing those boundaries so essential to a proper working relationship.

"Looks like we're tripping each other up," he said, his deep voice pitched so low it made the hair on her nape rise and her breasts tighten inside her corset, skin far too sensitive.

"I'm sorry," she said breathlessly. "I didn't mean

to get in your way," and yet she couldn't seem to step away, or give him space.

His hands wrapped around her upper arms and he gently but firmly lifted her, placing her back a foot, and then he exited the small cabin without a glance back.

Poppy exhaled in a rush, shuddering at the extreme awkwardness of what had just taken place. She'd walked into him, and then stayed there, planted, as if she'd become a tree and had grown miraculous roots.

Why?

Poppy carefully closed the door and then pressed her shoulder to the frame, wishing she could stay barricaded in the cabin forever. It was one thing to have an innocent crush on your boss, but it was another to want his touch, and Poppy wanted his touch. She wanted his hands on her in the worst sort of way. Which raised the question, what kind of person was she?

Poppy had always prided herself on her scruples. Well, where were they now?

CHAPTER THREE

POPPY STRUGGLED WITH the minute hooks on the pink dress, freeing herself little by little until she could wiggle out of the gown. The dress had been so tight that it had left livid pink marks all over her rib cage and breasts. It was bliss to finally be free and she slid the shirt on, buttoning the front. The fabric had been lightly starched and it rubbed against her nipples, making them tighten. She prayed Randall wouldn't notice. Things were already so awkward between them. She'd always thought they had the ideal relationship, professional but warm, cordial and considerate, but today had changed everything.

Today he overwhelmed her, and her brain told her to run but there was another part of her that desperately wanted to stay.

And be touched.

That was a very worrying part of her.

She'd have to work hard to keep that part in check, because elegant, refined Randall Grant was one thing, but dark, brooding Dal Grant was something else altogether.

Poppy finished changing, stepping into the soft, faded jeans that now hung on her hips thanks to four months of determined dieting, and after pulling the pins from her hair, she slipped her feet into her tennis shoes and headed back to her seat.

While she was gone, the flight attendant added a low arrangement of flowers to the center of the table, the lush red and pink roses reminiscent of the bouquet Sophie had carried this morning. The flowers made Poppy heartsick and guilty all over again.

"You look more comfortable," he said as she slid into her seat.

"I am."

"Tell me your sizes and I'll have some basics waiting for us when we land."

"I can shop for myself, thank you."

"There won't be shops where we're going."

"Where are we going?"

"Jolie."

The flight attendant appeared with the salad course, and Poppy waited for Randall to reach for his fork before she did the same. "Is it a country house?" she asked.

He didn't pick up his fork, or answer right away, instead he glanced away, his long black lashes lowering, accenting the high, hard lines of his cheekbones.

She'd always thought he had the most impressive bone structure, with his lovely high cheekbones, strong jaw and chin coupled with that long nose. Sophie had always disdained of his nose—not refined enough— but Poppy had disagreed, thinking he had the nose of a Roman or Greek.

"Something like that," he finally answered, his dark head turning, his light gold gaze returning to her, studying her for a long moment, making her feel strangely light-headed. And breathless. Far too breathless.

Poppy inhaled slowly, trying to settle her nerves. She'd had a crush on him for four years and she'd managed to keep her feelings in check. There was no reason to let herself get carried away just because he was suddenly single.

And free.

Her heart did a funny little beat, the kind of beat that made her feel anxious and excited, but neither emotion was useful. She needed to settle down and be calm and steady and strong.

"You're not doing much to clarify things." She tried to smile, a steady, professional smile. "Where is it exactly?"

"Out of the country."

Did he just say out *in* the country, or out *of* the country? It was a tiny preposition, but a significant difference. "Where is the nearest airport?"

"Gila."

She touched the tip of her tongue to her upper lip as her mouth had gone dry and her stomach was doing a wild free fall. "I'm not familiar with Gila."

"The capital of Mehkar?"

For a moment she still didn't understand, unable to process what he was saying, and then everything inside her did a horrifying free fall. "We're going to *Mehkar*?"

"Have you been before?"

"No."

"It neighbors Morocco—"

"I know where it is, but we can't go to Mehkar!"

"Of course we can. We're en route now."

"But how? Why? It's hours away and I have no passport, just an overnight bag with virtually nothing in it at all."

He shrugged carelessly. "Sophie had nothing when she left the church, did she?"

Poppy's throat sealed closed and she stared at Randall, heartsick. He stared right back, his light gold gaze hard, so hard that it made him look like a stranger.

"You're not worried about her, are you?" he added, his voice dropping, deepening, an edge of menace in his tone.

A shiver raced through her. In the past hour Randall Grant had gone from chivalrous to dangerous.

"Answer me," Randall demanded, leaning forward, his anger altogether new. The Randall Grant she knew was impossibly calm, impossibly controlled.

"I didn't agree to leave the country," she said, voice rising, tightening. "I didn't agree to go to Mehkar. I'd like to return to London immediately. I have work to do—"

"You work for me."

"But the work I need to do for you is all there," she said, making a jabbing motion behind them. "So, please ask your captain to turn around and take me back to Winchester, or to London, so I can take care of the one hundred and one things that need to be done by Monday."

"You can do them in Mehkar."

"But I can't."

"You can, and you will, because it's your job to handle this crushing mountain of work I've tasked you with."

"I never said it was crushing."

"You make it sound crushing."

"I do have a lot of responsibility, and I take my work seriously. Nor do I want to let you down."

His firm lips quirked, but it wasn't a friendly smile.

"I don't think that's true at all." His gaze slowly traveled across her face, as if examining every inch. "In fact, I know it's not true."

Heat rushed through her and she felt every place his gaze touched grow uncomfortably warm. "No?"

"No." He was about to add something else, but the flight attendant appeared to remove their salad plates even though neither of them had barely touched the greens.

Randall remained silent the entire time she was gone, and stayed silent while their next course was placed before them. Poppy stared down at her seafood risotto, feeling increasingly queasy. Seafood risotto was Sophie's favorite, not hers. Poppy didn't like seafood, or risotto.

She looked up at Randall to discover that he was watching her intently, his dark head tipped back against the pale leather seat, lids lowering, lashes dropping, concealing part of the golden glimmer. "If you valued your position with me, Poppy, you would be loyal to me. Yet, you're not."

For a second it seemed as if all the oxygen in the plane disappeared and she stared at him, lips parting, but no air moving in or out of her lungs. No air, and no words, either, because what could she say? How could she defend herself?

"Have you found a new position, Poppy?"

She shook her head, eyes stinging.

"Are you interviewing?"

She shook her head again.

"Résumés out…inquiries…networking?"

Poppy's stomach twisted. "No. I am not job-hunting. I like my job."

"Is that so?"

"Yes."

"Then maybe it's time you showed me some loyalty, Poppy Marr, and tell me what you know about Sophie and this Crisanti fellow."

She deserved that. Because she had taken sides, hadn't she? She'd taken Sophie's. Sophie was her best friend. Her only friend. If Sophie was queen, Poppy would be her lady in waiting. "I would like to help you," she said, stomach still churning, nerves and nausea. It didn't help that the smell of the risotto was making her want to gag. She carefully pushed her bowl away. "But I don't really know much of anything."

His set expression indicated he didn't believe her. "But you know something," he said. "So let's start with that. How long has Sophie known Crisanti? Where did she meet him?"

"I don't want to do this, and it's not fair of you to ask me when you know Sophie is the only one who has ever looked out for me—"

"Are you saying I haven't?"

He'd spoken lowly and yet his words vibrated all the way through her. She clutched the edge of the table, panicked and overwhelmed, not simply by what he was asking, but by the unreality of their situation.

She'd harbored the crush for years, falling for him almost from the very start as he was handsome and intelligent and wildly successful and best of all, he was kind to her, and always so very thoughtful, mindful of her feelings even when things were stressful at work.

It was on one of those terribly stressful days that Poppy had overshared with him, blurting out her fears and insecurities that she'd always be single, because men wanted women like Sophie, women who were strong and confident, women that made men feel like men.

Randall had sputtered on muffled laughter and then he shook his head, eyes smiling. "You can't compare yourself to Sophie. That's not fair of you. Sophie is Sophie Carmichael-Jones for a reason. There's only one of her, but also, there is only one of you. The key, Poppy Marr, is to be you."

"I don't think that's enough," she answered tearfully.

"Trust me, it's more than enough."

And as he'd looked at her, his gold eyes still smiling, she'd melted into a puddle of aching gratitude, want and wishful dreams. *Imagine* having Randall Grant as your champion. Imagine him in your corner, as your partner. Poppy had never been more envious of Sophie in all her life.

Poppy swallowed hard now, a lump in her throat. "You've always been very, very kind to me. Probably better than I deserve."

"So why only protect Sophie? Why not try to protect me?"

"But I did!" she choked. "I wasn't just trying to help Sophie. I was trying to help you, too!"

"So how did you help us?" he asked softly, silkily. "What did you do?"

He'd done it. He'd trapped her, cornered her, and she'd all but confessed.

Horrified, Poppy tried to run, but Randall caught her by the wrist as she attempted to leave the table. His fingers tightened around her slender bones, and he pulled her toward his side.

"Tell me," he said quietly, tugging her closer to his chair. "Let's have the truth."

She tried to pull free, but he was so much stronger than she was, and then he began to stroke the inside of her wrist with his thumb, lightly running the pad of his thumb over her wildly beating pulse. It was the most electric sensation, her nerves jumping, dancing, sending little rivulets of feeling everywhere.

"Sit," he said, drawing her toward him, and then pulling her down so that she perched on the arm of his chair. "Talk. The truth now."

But how could she think, much less say anything coherent, when his thumb was caressing her wrist, making her tingle all over?

She looked up into his eyes and her breath caught as she saw something in his eyes she'd never seen before.

Heat. A fierce, raw, masculine heat that was completely at odds with the man she knew.

But then his thumb caressing her pulse was equally at odds with Randall Grant, the Earl of Langston. The Earl of Langston was elegant, disciplined, restrained. The Earl of Langston did not want *her*.

"I can't think when you're doing that," she said under her breath.

"And I can't have you running off every time the questions get uncomfortable." He moved his hand, sliding it from her wrist up over the flat of her hand so that they were palm to palm, his long fingers pressing against hers, parting them.

She shivered at the press of his hand to hers. It felt wildly indecent.

"I would say this is far more uncomfortable than any of your questions," she whispered, trying to slip her hand out, but only succeeding in dragging her palm down his, sending sparks of sensation up her arm, through her breasts and into her belly below.

His fingers laced through hers, holding her still.

She looked down at their joined hands because there was no way she could look into his face right now. "I don't think this is proper."

"It's a little late to worry about propriety, Poppy. So tell me what you did. You don't need to tell me why. I think we both know the why."

She closed her eyes, mortified, not sure if he was suggesting what she thought he was suggesting.

She prayed he wasn't suggesting...

She prayed...

Just then the plane lurched and dropped, caught in a violent stream of turbulence, and Randall clamped his arm over her thighs, his hand locking around her knee, holding her steady. "I have you," he said.

And he did, she thought wildly, eyes opening as heat and desire rushed through her.

He'd touched her before—a hand to her elbow as he assisted her across a gravel car park, or a touch to her shoulder when entering a crowded lift to nudge her forward—but never like this. Never anything like this, and she was suddenly riveted by the sight of his hand on her knee, his fingers as lean and strong and elegant as the rest of him.

She'd imagined this, though, hadn't she?

Poppy smashed the little voice but it was too late, the little voice wouldn't be silenced. It was beyond inappropriate to have feelings for him in the first place. Randall Grant was Sophie's fiancé and her employer, and Poppy would rather cut off her right arm than embarrass Sophie, or Randall. But that didn't mean the feelings weren't there, suppressed. Buried.

She worked hard to keep them mashed down, too. And one of the ways she contained her feelings was by keeping a proper distance from him.

She didn't let herself stand too close, or bend too low.

She didn't look him in the eye more than was necessary.

She dressed conservatively, even frumpishly, so no one could accuse her of trying to play up her assets—not that there were too many of those.

And she called him Randall, not Dal like his other friends, because she wasn't his friend. She was his secretary and on his payroll, and those were key distinctions.

She couldn't ever risk forgetting herself.

She couldn't risk dropping her guard, letting him see that beneath her professional demeanor was a real woman…a woman who wanted nothing more than to see him happy. Because Randall Grant was many things—brilliant, wealthy, strategic, successful—but he wasn't happy. In fact, he didn't seem to allow himself to feel emotions at all.

Perhaps that was what troubled her most. He would give the shirt off his back to someone in need, but he never asked for anything in return.

He never took anything from anyone, or wanted anything for himself.

He just existed in his space and sphere, brilliant and handsome and impossibly solitary.

Sophie had never seemed to notice. In her mind, Dal was just one of those introverts…a loner…and content to be alone, but Poppy didn't agree. Of course she kept her opinion to herself. But instinct told her that Randall Grant hadn't always been so alone, and that his isolation was perhaps the result of his being raised by a difficult father.

"I think you should let me go, Randall." Her voice was soft, almost broken.

"Maybe, but I don't think I shall. I quite like having you close. You have no defenses right now, making it impossible for you to lie."

"You're more of a gentleman than that."

"Oh, Poppy, you don't know me at all."

"That's not so. I know you quite well—"

"You've made me into someone I never was. Your impression of me is sweet, and flattering, but absurdly false. I am no gentleman, and am anything but chivalrous."

"I'd like to return to my chair now."

"Why? Isn't this what you always wanted? Haven't you wondered what it would be like to be Sophie, engaged to me?"

Poppy stiffened. She couldn't move, or blink, or speak. She couldn't do anything but sit frozen while shame suffused her heart. *He knew?* Dear God, did he really know? All these years she'd thought she'd been so good at hiding her feelings, hiding her attraction, and yet apparently she hadn't hidden anything well at all.

But then she forced the thought back, not willing to go there, not willing to be stripped emotionally bare before him. "How much whiskey did you drink?" she flashed, praying he hadn't heard the wobble in her voice.

"The one glass. I'm not drunk." He leaned back

against his leather seat, infuriatingly relaxed. "And you can play it cool, and pretend you don't know what I'm talking about, but we both know the truth. I'm not trying to shame you—"

"It certainly feels like it, and I don't appreciate it. I was supposed to be going on holiday in the morning. I haven't had a proper vacation in years and this should have been the start to a vacation and instead you have me trapped on your plane, listening to your insults."

"It's not an insult."

"For you to imply that I've been dying for you to kiss me, yes, that's an insult because until five hours ago you were marrying my best friend."

"I never said Sophie knew. You were remarkably good at concealing your feelings when she was around."

"I don't have feelings for you!"

His expression of amused disbelief made her want to throw up.

"Can we agree on soft spot?" he suggested with the same insufferable smile.

Poppy shuddered. She averted her face, trying to hide behind her shoulder. "I miss the old you, the nice you. Can you please bring Randall Grant back?"

"Randall Grant is dead."

Her head jerked up and her gaze met his.

He nodded, expression almost sympathetic. "Yes, dead, because he never existed. I am Dal Grant, and have always been Dal. You made me into this Randall who was good and kind and considerate, but that's not me. It never has been."

"Fine. You're Dal Grant. Congratulations." She

yanked on her hand, struggling to free herself, struggling with a new, feverish desperation. "Now, let me go."

"Not yet."

"Why not?"

"Because we need to finish establishing a few things—"

"I think we've established quite a lot already. You're Dal, not Randall. You're not a nice man and you never have been. You think I betrayed you—"

"I *know* you betrayed me."

"And you want me to betray Sophie."

"But you don't want to do that."

"Of course I don't. And I won't."

"Because she was your champion. She protected you from the time you were just a charity case at Haskell's—"

"Stop, just stop."

"I understand more than you think I do. I know more than you think I do, too. I know you grew up poor and insecure, and how you believed that you had to be perfect, or close to perfect, because one misstep and you could lose it all. Your scholarship at Haskell's. Your friendship with Sophie. And then later, your job with me. Sophie once said that the reason you were so dependable was because you knew life was precarious and fraught with uncertainties. You'd told her that the best way to survive, and maybe the only way to survive, was by being necessary to those around you. So you became Sophie's rock. And then my rock."

"You were Sophie's rock, too," he continued, "but she's gone now, and that leaves just you and me."

She flushed deeply, even as her body throbbed with awareness. Randall's arm still lay across her thighs, and his hand continued to cup her knee, and her pulse was beating so hard that her head felt woozy. "I don't like the way you make that sound."

"How am I making it sound?"

"As if there is something…illicit…between us. But there is nothing illicit. There is just a work relationship, and this—" she broke off, gesturing to the chair and the place she sat "—is not proper or professional and I'm asking you to let me go so that I can return to my chair."

"Did you not invite Renzo to my wedding today?"

Her stomach rose and fell and she stared into Randall's golden eyes, stricken. Had Renzo contacted Randall? Had there been communication of some sort between the two men?

But no, that couldn't be. There was no way.

He was making wild guesses, trying to unsettle her, and it was unsettling, but he didn't know anything and she could not, absolutely could not, give him details. Let him speculate all he wanted, but it would be disastrous if she confirmed her part in today's debacle.

Stay calm, she told herself. *Don't panic.*

And don't feel, and don't think about how warm Randall's hand is, or how heat seemed to radiate from him to her, seeping into her skin, making her aware of how large his hands were, and how the pressure of his forearm across her thighs made her feel tingly, and tingly wasn't good. Tingly was dangerous.

"It's not disloyal to care for us both," he added after a moment.

"I won't say more. I'm done talking."

"I could get you to say more. I could get you right now to tell me everything." He must have seen her expression because his mouth eased and his eyes warmed. "One kiss—"

"For God's sake, stop!" Tears filled her eyes and reached up to wipe them away before they could fall. "I know you've had a bad day. I know this has to be one of the worst days of your life, but why must you torture me? I love Sophie, and I love you—"

She broke off, horrified to have said so much, to have admitted the depth of her feelings. She closed her eyes, teeth biting into her lower lip to keep it from trembling, and yet she couldn't stop the tears from falling, one after the other, but she gave up trying to catch them, or stop them.

It didn't matter.

Nothing mattered anymore.

"I quit," she whispered. "I'm done. Consider this my formal resignation. As of now, I no longer work for you and the moment we land, I'm gone."

CHAPTER FOUR

DAL RELEASED HER, and Poppy returned to her chair, but Dal was fully aware that she didn't eat anything, choosing to simply stare out the window, the very picture of martyred innocence.

But she wasn't innocent. She was responsible today for his being on this plane, now, a single man, and he wasn't just holding her accountable. He fully expected her to solve his problem, saving him from failing his father.

Dal had never been close to his father but he'd made a vow to his father when he was dying, and he fully intended to keep the promise.

Which meant, he needed a wife. Quickly.

Thank goodness Poppy was available. She wasn't the wife his father had wanted for him, but she'd definitely do in a pinch.

Sadie, the flight attendant, appeared to check on them and when she saw that neither of them had eaten the risotto she asked if there was something else she could bring.

"The cheese plates," Dal answered. "And whatever chocolates you might have. It's an emergency."

Poppy muttered something unflattering beneath her

breath and Dal looked at her, eyebrow rising. "You once said chocolate helps everything."

"Well, not *this*."

"I think you're wrong. I think once you eat some proper food and then have some excellent chocolate you'll calm down and realize you don't want to walk away from me in Mehkar, at the Gila airport—"

"Why not? It's supposed to be a gorgeous country."

"Without a passport, or money, or bra. Mehkar is not as conservative as some of our neighbors but it's still an Arab country with a traditional culture."

"I can't believe you felt the need to mention the bra."

"Men are men."

"Well then, once we land, and you get out, send me back to England in your plane. That way I won't be stranded and my lack of undergarments won't create alarm."

"And what will you do once you're back in London?"

"Go on the holiday. Sleep in. Enjoy the freedom of being unemployed."

"And then when you're properly rested you'll begin looking for a new job."

"Yes."

He studied her thoughtfully. "But won't it be hard to get a decent position without references? I'd think you'd need me to put in a good word for you. You did work for me for four years after all."

"That's not fair."

"What happened today in the chapel wasn't fair, either."

"Sophie always did say she knew you better than I thought. Clearly, she was right."

His secretary was so disillusioned that he almost felt sorry for her. "It will be better tomorrow."

"What will be?"

"The disappointment. You'll realize it's just a temporary setback, and life goes on."

Poppy glared at him, her brown eyes flashing. "Thank you for that extremely deep and insightful philosophy lecture."

Sadie returned with two cheese plates, each plate filled with cheeses, crackers and fruit, along with a bowl of chocolates. She set the plates down, centered the bowl of chocolate and disappeared.

Dal watched Poppy try to ignore the chocolates and cheese plate. It was almost comical because he knew how much she loved both things. "You really will feel better if you eat something."

She refused to look at him, her smooth jaw set, lips pursed, expression mutinous. He'd never seen this side of her. She had a temper. He was pleased to see it, too. He'd worried that she had no backbone. He'd worried that Sophie had taken advantage of her generous nature.

"There is no reason to continue the starvation diet," he said. "The wedding is over. No one is going to compare you to Sophie's stick friends."

Poppy gave him an indignant look. "They're not sticks. They're models."

"They're annoying."

"You really think so?"

"You've never noticed that they live on their phones? For them, social media is more important than real human interaction."

"It's because they get paid for their Instagram posts. The more likes they get, the bigger the bonuses."

He rolled his eyes. "I find that very hard to believe."

"It's true. I didn't know it until one of them explained that modeling has changed. Lots of their jobs are pictures for their Instagram accounts."

"I'm still not impressed."

"Are you being serious? You really didn't like them?"

"Did you?" he retorted.

He seemed to have caught Poppy off guard and she paused to think about her answer. After a moment her shoulders shrugged. "They were nice enough to me."

"But?"

"I wasn't one of them."

"Of course not. You weren't an actress or a model—"

"Some of them are just horsey girls. They live for polo."

"You mean, rich men who play polo."

"You don't sound very complimentary."

"I knew I was marrying Sophie, not her social scene."

Poppy regarded him for another long moment, her wide brown eyes solemn, her full mouth compressed, and he was glad she was nothing like Sophie's other friends. He was glad she was short and curvy and fresh-faced and real. She was Poppy. And she was maybe the only person in his life who could make him smile.

"But maybe that was part of the problem," she said now, picking her words with care. "Maybe you needed to like her world better. Sophie is quite social. She likes going out and doing things. She was never going to be happy sitting around Langston House with you every weekend."

"It's a wonderful house."

"For you. It's your house. But what was she supposed to do there all day?" When he didn't answer she pressed on. "Have you ever looked at her? Really looked at her? Sophie is one of the most beautiful, stylish women in all of England. *Tatler* adores her—"

He made a dismissive noise.

Poppy ignored him. "Everyone in the fashion world adores her. Sophie is smart and glamorous and she is very much admired, but you…you only saw her as the woman who would beget your heirs."

When Dal's mocking smile disappeared Poppy felt a stab of pleasure, delighted that she knocked his smug, arrogant smile off his smug, arrogant, albeit handsome, face, but then when he rose and walked away, the pleasure abruptly faded.

Chewing the inside of her lip, she watched him walk to the back, heading for his private cabin in the rear of the jet. After he disappeared into the cabin, the door closing soundlessly behind him, she sank back into her seat, deflated, as if all the energy had been sucked from the cabin.

So much had just happened that she couldn't process it all.

Poppy didn't even know where to begin taking apart the conversations and the revelations, never mind examining the intense emotions buffeting her.

Randall—Dal—knew about her infatuation, and had implied that Sophie probably knew, too. And then Poppy, in a burst of uncharacteristic temper, had quit.

Poppy sighed and rubbed her brow, gently kneading the ache. Was she really going to leave him, after four years of working for him? After four years of trying to deny her feelings?

And did it matter that he knew her secret?

On one hand it was incredibly uncomfortable that Randall—Dal—knew, but on the other, so what?

She had feelings for him. Why should that make her feel ashamed? Why were feelings even considered shameful? She'd been emotional in her entire life. From the time she was a little girl, she'd felt things intensely. Her sensitive nature had made her a target for the girls at Haskell's. They'd enjoyed teasing her about being a charity case. They'd enjoyed mocking her lack of coordination and athletic ability. They'd enjoyed her discomfort at being forced to remain at school for holidays because her parents couldn't afford to bring her home.

And then wonderful, lovely, courageous Sophie stepped in and made the teasing and bullying stop. But she didn't just make the teasing stop; Sophie changed Poppy's life when she confessed that she respected Poppy's kindness and good heart. Suddenly, Poppy wasn't embarrassing but someone that Sophie Carmichael-Jones admired.

So of course Poppy had never acted on her feelings for Randall. She would never, ever be disloyal to Sophie. At the same time, what harm had there been secretly caring for Randall? Her devotion made her a better assistant. Her dedication making her more sensitive and attuned to his needs.

But now her secret was in the open. Did it have to change everything? Did she *want* it to change anything?

Did she want to say goodbye to Randall?

Poppy didn't know the answer to the first two questions but she knew the answer to the third. She didn't want to leave Randall. And the way she felt about him, she'd never want to leave him, but how could she continue working for him like this?

It wouldn't be the same. She'd feel self-conscious and he'd be awkward. Better to end things while she still cared about him. Better to say goodbye while she wanted the best for him.

But just admitting that she had to go broke her heart.

Dal closed his computer, rose from his desk and put away the computer in his briefcase. The jet had just begun the final descent for Gila and he'd not only canceled the essential pieces of the honeymoon but had also created a short list of possible countess candidates to share with Poppy when he returned to the main cabin.

The list was for show. There was only one woman he was considering to be his wife, and that was his secretary, but if he told Poppy she was the one and only name, she'd be terrified. Far better to ease her into her new reality, and it would be her reality because Dal had to be married by the time he turned thirty-five, and his birthday was just sixteen days away.

Which meant he had sixteen days to find a new bride and marry her as he wasn't going to lose Langston House, or the earldom, or any of the other Grant estates, because he'd failed his father.

He'd grown up with enough abuse. He wasn't going to let his father win, even if he was in the grave.

So he'd marry Poppy and prove his father wrong and then Dal would finally be free of this burden he'd carried that he wasn't his brother Andrew, and that he wasn't fit to be the Earl of Langston, and he didn't deserve the Langston House and estates.

Now he just needed to convince her that she was the perfect future countess.

Dal left the back office and returned to his seat in the main cabin. As he took his seat, Poppy stirred sleepily in her chair. Her lashes fluttered open for a moment before closing again. "You," she murmured crossly.

"Yes, me," he answered, his gaze sweeping her, studying her for the first time in an entirely different light.

She wasn't his secretary anymore, but his future wife, which meant not just overseeing Langston House and the thousand different domestic tasks that encompassed, but also bearing him the necessary Grant heirs.

It wouldn't be difficult taking her to his bed. She was pretty and tidy and wholesome, although at the moment she looked flushed and rumpled from sleep, her brown hair down tumbling to her shoulders while a rebellious tendril clung to her pink cheek.

His dress shirt overwhelmed her small frame, but it was refreshing seeing her in something other than her conservative navy and brown skirts, which she paired with equally conservative cardigans. In warm weather she swapped the jumpers for trim white blouses with oval collars and half sleeves. Her work wardrobe was neither well cut nor flattering, and while the pinstripe shirt wasn't flattering, it revealed her curves. Poppy Marr was voluptuous with hourglass curves. Full breasts, tiny waist, rounded hips. He suddenly wished she wasn't wearing jeans so he could see her legs. He'd very much like to see her in nothing but his shirt, and then without the shirt altogether.

"What do you want now?" she demanded, stretching and covering a yawn.

"We should be landing soon."

"Good."

He'd never noticed how firm her chin was until now. It matched her new backbone. He liked the spirit. Spirit was sexy and strong and his future countess would need to be strong.

"I'm not sending you back to England," he said casually. "You owe me two weeks after giving notice. It's in your employment agreement. You can't just quit and walk away."

Her dark lashes slowly lifted and she stared at him, clearly unhappy. "You're going on holiday. You don't need me."

"I'm not on holiday, and I do need you."

"For what?"

"To help find your replacement. I can't possibly interview for a new secretary and a new wife at the same time."

She stared at him blankly. "You're already trying to replace Sophie?"

"She's gone, isn't she?"

"Isn't that rather…callous?"

"Did you expect me to mourn her?"

"She was loyal to you for five and a half years!"

"But she decamped at the last possible second, and the fact is, I need a wife, quickly."

"You've never needed anyone, and yet now you must have a wife, immediately."

"It does sound ridiculous put like that, but that pretty much sums it up."

"I don't understand."

"It's a very convoluted story so I'll give you the short version. I must be married by my thirty-fifth birthday or I lose the earldom, the house and everything attached."

She was still for a moment before she sat upright in her chair. "Your birthday is July sixteenth."

"Correct."

"That's just...a few weeks away."

"Correct again."

She impatiently shoved hair behind an ear, away from her flushed cheek. "This sounds like something from a novel."

"I'm fully aware of the ridiculousness of my situation, but my father set up the trust that way. When he died just after my thirtieth birthday, I inherited the title, but there were provisions."

Silence followed his words. Poppy looked absolutely appalled.

Dal shrugged, adding. "My father thought he was being clever. Exerting control from beyond the grave, and so forth."

"When did you find out? At the reading of the will?"

"No, although wouldn't that have been a shock? Surprised my father didn't think of that. But no, I've known since my early twenties, and did my best not to think about it until I was nearly thirty."

"Did Sophie know this?"

"Sophie was part of my father's plan. He hand-selected her for me."

"This just keeps getting worse."

"She didn't ever tell you?"

"Heavens, no. But probably because she knew I'd

disapprove. No wonder she ran at the last second. I would run, too. Poor Sophie."

"Sophie benefitted from the arrangement…until she didn't." He shrugged carelessly. "But now there is a serious time crunch. I have to be married in sixteen days. It's hard enough closing a big deal in two weeks, but to find a wife in the same amount of time? It's not going to be easy."

"And there is no way out of this?"

"No. But trust me, I tried. I've spent a fortune in legal fees and finally accepted that marriage really is the only solution."

She bit her lip and looked away, a sheen of tears in her eyes. "I am so upset."

In his shirt, with her thick hair loose and her slim legs curled up in the seat of her chair, she exuded youth and a sweet, innocent sensuality that teased his senses.

"Don't be," he answered her, forcing his attention from her lips to the sweep of her cheekbone and the strands of dark hair framing her pale oval face. "There is no point in both of us being upset."

"I know I shouldn't say it, but the more I learn about your father, the more I dislike him."

"He was a very tortured man."

"It sounds as if he did his best to torture you."

This was not a comfortable conversation. Dal couldn't even remember the last time he'd discussed his father with anyone. "I'd like to believe it wasn't intentional. I'd like to think he just…couldn't help himself."

She rubbed her eyes and drew a deep breath and turned to look at him, focused now on the goal. "So you need a wife."

"Yes."

"Have you given thought to possible women you could see…proposing to?"

"Yes. I've thought about it carefully and made a short list." He reached into his pocket and pulled out the sheet of paper where he'd scrawled the names, handing it to her.

He sat back, studying her face as she skimmed the list. For a moment her expression was blank and then her head shot up, her rounded eyes matching her dropped jaw.

"I don't appreciate the joke," she said shortly, folding the sheet of paper in half and thrusting it back at him. "Take it."

"I couldn't be more serious."

"Obviously you don't really mean to marry in the next two weeks."

"Why not? You don't think any of the three could be suitable?"

"Perhaps the first two," she said bitingly, "but not the third. She's not rich or a Sloane Ranger."

He unfolded the sheet of paper and glanced down at the three names.

Seraphina Woolton
Florrie Goodwin
Poppy Marr

"But number three is smart and generous and easy to like," he answered, rereading the names.

"That would be very nice if you were a vicar, or a primary school teacher, but you're not. You're from one of the oldest, most prominent families in England and you need an appropriate wife, someone sophisticated, respected and connected."

"I do?"

"Obviously. It's what your father dictated, and it explains why you and Sophie had all those contracts and agreements."

"Yes, but that was with Sophie, and exclusive to my engagement to her. There is nothing that stipulates who my replacement bride should be."

"You started with a very small list, and it's just grown shorter as we're crossing number three off."

"Are we?"

"Yes. Poppy Marr is not an option, which means we'll need to focus on Seraphina and Florrie."

"But Poppy Marr *is* an option. All three names on that list are options. I thought quite seriously about each possible candidate—"

"Please don't use the word *candidate*. It's dreadful. It's as if you're trying to hire a woman to fill a position."

"Being the Countess of Langston is a job."

"Then definitely take Poppy Marr off your list. She's not interested in that position."

"Why not? We work well together."

"Because this new *job* requires skills that are outside my area of expertise." Her cheeks flamed and her eyes glowed bright. "Nor have I any interest in acquiring the skills necessary to be the Countess of Langston."

Heat surged through him, and he hardened as he pictured her fulfilling her marital duties. His trousers grew uncomfortably tight as he imagined introducing her to those duties. "I would teach you."

"*No.*"

"I'd be patient."

"We're ending this discussion now. It's not going to happen. It's not even a remote possibility. I'm not interested in jumping from your office to your bedroom. I like the you in your office."

"Randall," he said dismissively.

"Yes, Randall. Polite, controlled, chivalrous. I don't trust Dal at all."

"That's probably wise."

"Excuse me. Who are you? I don't even know you anymore!"

"I suspect it's because you never did."

"If that's the case, does anyone know you?"

His wry smile faded. That was an excellent question, and he had to think about it for a minute before answering. "Probably not."

More silence followed, and then Poppy broke it with a heavy sigh. "You have no idea how sad that makes me."

"And you, my dear Poppy Marr, have just moved into melodrama."

"Just because I feel things doesn't mean I'm being melodramatic."

"I have found that emotions unnecessarily complicate things."

"Probably because you were taught that emotions were bad things."

"No one has ever told me anything about emotions. My views are based on firsthand experience. Excessive emotion is toxic and damaging."

"What about good emotions? What about love and joy and—"

"That's Gila in the distance," he said mildly, cutting off her impassioned stream of words. "You can see the skyline on the horizon."

She shot him an indignant look, letting him know that she didn't appreciate him interrupting her, before craning her head to see out the window.

He watched as the city loomed nearer, surprisingly eager to see how much he recognized of the Mehkar capital. He'd heard that elegant, historic Gila had become a new, modern, urban city, but the change hadn't registered until now when he saw the dozens of new skyscrapers dotting the skyline.

As they approached the airport, they flew over lakes and glittering pools, and oases of green amidst the marble and glass. The captain turned just before they neared the historic neighborhoods, the ones Dal knew best as it was home to the royal palace, the place where his mother had grown up.

His mother loved to show off her hometown when they used to visit every year. They never went to Kasbah Jolie without first visiting their grandfather and family in Gila. One of their grandfather's drivers would take them out in one of the classic cars he loved, and they'd travel the wide, pristine boulevards lined with stately palm trees, boulevards that led to museums and palaces as well as her favorite shopping district.

To a boy, Gila represented family and history and culture. It never crossed his mind that it was a playground to others—sensual, sexy, hedonistic. It wasn't until he was at Cambridge that his friends talked about going to Mehkar on holiday, that Gila with its white marble and endless man-made lakes, was nonstop entertainment. His friends never understood why Dal wouldn't want to go on holiday to an exotic desert country famous for its hotels, restaurants, shopping and nightlife.

"I had no idea Gila was so big," Poppy said after a moment.

"There has been a lot of new development in the past twenty years. The people of Mehkar love their sports, and their toys."

"Sophie's friends used to come here for the polo tournaments."

"But not Sophie?"

"No. She always said she wanted to visit. Mehkar was on her bucket list." Poppy gave him one of her reproving looks. "But you should have known that, though. You were her fiancé, and engaged forever."

"Not forever, just five and a half years."

"Which is pretty much forever to a twenty-six-year-old." She continued to frown at him. "If you didn't discuss travel, and bucket lists, what *did* you discuss?"

He didn't immediately reply. The jet was dropping lower, and faster, a rapid descent, which meant they'd be on the ground soon before making the quick transfer to his helicopter, and Poppy would be making the transfer with him, too.

"Sophie and I didn't talk a lot. But I think you know that," he said as the wheels touched down in an impossibly smooth landing. They were still streaking down the runway, but soon they'd begin to slow.

"You can't blame her," Poppy answered. "Sophie wanted to be closer to you. You just wouldn't let her in."

And that was also probably true, he thought, but he didn't want to continue discussing Sophie. Sophie was part of the past. She'd chosen a different path, a different future, and it was time for him to focus on his future.

The jet turned at the end of the runway and began

the slow taxi toward the small, sleek, glass and steel terminal.

"Women feel close through word and language. We bond through talking—"

"I'm not ready for another lecture on emotions," he interrupted firmly in the authoritative voice he used when he needed to redirect Poppy, and he needed to redirect her now.

"I'm trying to help you."

"That may be the case, but I'm not in the right frame of mind to be presented with my overwhelming failures as a man."

"You're not a failure. But you could work on your emotional intelligence—"

"Poppy!"

She pressed her lips together, her expression defiant, and he drew a deep breath, trying to hang on to his patience.

"I thought you said you had only sixteen days to find a wife," she said in a small but still defiant voice.

Where had this new Poppy come from? She was beyond stubborn, and while he appreciated persistence, now was not the time. She had no idea how unsettled he felt. It was difficult returning to Mehkar. He was already dreading getting off the plane and transferring to the helicopter. Mehkar represented his mother and his carefree summer holidays with his brother at Jolie. He'd never truly dealt with their deaths. He'd just stopped thinking about them and now he was thinking about them and it wasn't a good day to be feeling overwhelmed.

Dammit.

Why had he thought that going to Kasbah Jolie was a good idea?

How had he thought this could be positive?

He shouldn't have come. He should have stayed put at Langston House and weathered the media storm and focused on wooing Poppy there. Instead, he was here, jumping from the proverbial fire into the frying pan.

Dal could see the helicopter ahead. He also saw the cars and the crowd and the royal security details. The black helicopter wasn't just any helicopter but the royal Mehkar helicopter, the elegant gold crest as familiar to him as his mother's face and name. His heart thudded, his chest tight and hard as he battled memories and a past that gave him nothing but pain.

Maybe one day he'd be able to remember his mother without feeling the grief. Maybe after he'd spent a week at Jolie he'd be more peaceful when he thought of Mehkar. In his teens he used to dream of the summer palace and gardens, and when he woke up, his lashes would be damp and his stomach cramping as though he'd swallowed glass.

All through his twenties he'd continued to miss his mother profoundly. He'd missed his brother, too, but it was his mother that he had been closest to. His mother had been the anchor when his father struggled. Andrew had somehow been able to block out their father's volatility, but Dal, the sensitive second son, hadn't been able to unplug from the drama and chaos.

Dal wasn't proud of the boy he'd been. Sensitive boys were no good to anyone and it took his father ten years to stomp the sensitivity out of him, but Dal survived, and became a man, and a relatively successful, stable man.

The jet came to a stop. His flight attendant, Sadie, rose from her seat to open the door. But Dal didn't move, not yet ready.

He turned to Poppy, who was reaching for her seat belt. "So we're in agreement, then? You give me the full two weeks I'm due, and then if you still want to leave, I'll personally put you on a plane home. But I need the two weeks, and I need you available, round the clock if need be."

Poppy's gaze met his. She held his gaze, too, not afraid to let him see the full measure of her disapproval. "Round the clock sounds excessive. I'm not your nursemaid, I'm your secretary. And at the end of the two weeks, I will most definitely still go, so don't just focus on finding your wife. Work on the replacement for me, too."

"I trust you to find me a suitable secretary."

"You're leaving the entire task to me?"

"You know what I like, and what I need."

Her brows arched over her clear brown eyes. "You might regret this."

"Possibly. But I'm in a bind, Poppy, and you're the only one that can save me."

"Now you're laying it on a tad thick."

The corner of his mouth lifted. "You like to be needed."

Two spots of color burned in her cheeks. "But I draw the line at becoming a business transaction."

He said nothing and silence stretched and yet she never once looked away.

"I don't think I've ever refused you anything," she said after a moment, "but I am now. I won't be manipulated. You have two weeks and then I'm gone."

* * *

It had taken every bit of Poppy's courage and strength to stand up to Randall—Dal—and define her terms, because if she didn't make it absolutely clear, then she'd find it very hard to resist him.

It had nearly melted her when he'd said he needed her. She liked being needed, and once upon a time, she would have given everything to hear him say that he needed *her*.

But things had changed, circumstances had changed, and she couldn't continue in his employment, not when he knew she had feelings for him. He'd use the knowledge to his advantage. He'd be able to manipulate her far too easily.

As it was, he was intimidating. Not frightening intimidating, but thrilling. He was so very handsome, and so very polished and so very accomplished.

Every time he entered a room, he seemed to light it up. She loved the way he moved, and the way he frowned and the way he'd focus on whatever he was reading.

She loved the way he held his teacup—

Oh, heavens, she loved him. She did. And it had been excruciating trying to manage her feelings and her attraction when he'd been engaged to Sophie. How could she possibly manage her envy and jealousy as he began to court someone new? She'd hate the new woman. She'd resent her far too much. It wouldn't be comfortable for any of them.

Poppy rose from her seat and smoothed her men's shirt, and then her hair, tucking it behind her ears to control the thick wave.

Dal was leaving the jet, descending the stairs, and

she kept her eyes on his broad shoulders as she followed him down the five steps and onto the wide red carpet banded by gold. The brilliant crimson carpet was something of a shock, but even more surprising was the sheer number of people gathered on the tarmac.

There were rows of robed men, and then rows of armed men, and even a couple of men with what looked like musical instruments.

Dal, for his part, did not look pleased by the welcome. From the set of his shoulders and the rigid line of his back, she knew he was tense and angry. She fully expected him to step onto the carpet and proceed toward the helicopter. Instead, he turned to her and offered his hand, to aid her down the last few steps.

She felt a little silly accepting his help when she was wearing jeans and tennis shoes, not the staggeringly high heels Sophie preferred. But his fingers closed around hers, and he gave her hand a quick, reassuring squeeze as she stepped from the stairs onto the carpet.

And then he let her hand go and he started walking down the carpet, which stretched from the plane to the side of a huge black helicopter with a gold emblem on the helicopter's door. The same gold emblem filled the middle of the crimson carpet, and two rows of men in long white robes and headwear stood on either side of the carpet.

It was intimidating as hell, she thought, swallowing nervously, picking up her pace to catch up to him. "Dal," she whispered, taking in the men farther back, the armed ones, with their big guns and vests and helmets. "Who are all these people?"

"The welcoming committee," he answered.

Well, the welcoming committee was bowing now

to Dal, every head nodding as he passed. A shiver coursed through her as she trailed after him. It was the strangest greeting she'd ever seen, and beyond formal, reminding her of the ceremony reserved for England's royal family.

Poppy didn't know what Randall had done to earn such a welcoming, or what the emblem of sword, lamb and crown represented, but clearly the government of Mehkar was aware of his arrival today, and clearly the government of Mehkar wanted Dal to know they respected him.

At the helicopter Randall stopped and clasped hands with a robed man that looked close to Randall's age. The man said something to Randall in a foreign language, and Randall answered in the same language, and then they shook hands, and the handshake became a swift hug, and then the hug became a longer, warmer embrace.

When Randall stepped back, there was a sheen in his golden eyes, and a flicker of emotion that Poppy had never seen before. But then the emotion was gone and Randall's features were hard, and his expression remote. He assisted Poppy into the helicopter and she glanced back at the men Randall had called a welcoming committee, and it was only then that she noticed the rows of cars farther back, black limousines with tinted windows.

"That was quite impressive," she said, sliding into the seat by the far window and reaching for the harness.

"It was," he agreed as the pilot shut the helicopter door.

She felt dazed by the pomp and ceremony. "Who do you have to know to get a welcoming like that?"

"The king."

Her eyes widened. "He's one of the men you work with?"

"In my international work? No. My relationship with King Hamid is personal. I've known him my whole life." Randall hesitated. "King Hamid is my mother's father."

It took her a second to put the pieces together. "He's your *grandfather.*"

Randall nodded once. "My mother's father."

"That's why you received such a royal welcome."

"Here in Mehkar I am not Randall Grant, the Sixth Earl of Langston, but rather Sheikh Talal bin Mehkar."

It had been a day of shocks and surprises and this one was just as stunning. Poppy stared at him, bewildered. "You're a…*sheikh*?"

CHAPTER FIVE

POPPY'S HEAD THROBBED, the thumping at the base of her skull making her feel as if her head would soon explode. He was a sheikh *and* an earl? How was it possible?

Furthermore, how could she not know? Did *anyone* know?

It was one thing not to know that he had a private jet stashed in London, but another not to know his mother was a princess from Mehkar!

But thinking about it, Poppy realized she'd never read anything in the papers about his mother's family. There was very little in the society magazines about who she was, or where she came from, and Poppy knew because she used to read everything she could on Dal, and there were stories about his father, and his father's family, and lots of stories about Langston House itself, but very little about his mother. Some articles did briefly mention the tragic car accident that took the life of his mother and brother, but that was all that was ever said.

Now Poppy wondered if it was the Fifth Earl of Langston who'd kept his wife's name from the papers, or if it had been the royal family of Mehkar?

Poppy glanced at Dal. He was giving that impression of stone again, the same look he'd had this morning in the chapel. Detached. Immovable. It wasn't really a good look. It made her worry even more. "Dal?"

"Mmm?"

"Are you okay?"

"Never better," he answered mockingly.

She sighed and looked out the window, her stomach doing a little free fall when she did.

She'd been in helicopters before. She'd traveled with Randall in his helicopter dozens of times over the years, accompanying him to meetings, taking notes, pulling together his travel details, but the London-based helicopter was small compared to this one, and that one never flew over jagged mountains marked by narrow, deep ravines.

She tried not to look down. She didn't want to see just how close they were to the mountains, or how far from civilization, either.

There was nothing here.

Just scrub brush. The occasional flock of sheep. What seemed to be a sheepherder's hut made of mud and stacked stone.

Poppy exhaled softly, fingers curling into her palms, telling herself to relax. Not worry. But how could she not be concerned? The Randall Grant she thought she knew was gone, and this new man was even more complex and mysterious. "I know you said you didn't want to discuss Sophie anymore," she said carefully.

"Right."

"But I've been thinking about what you said, and how you feel betrayed by both Sophie and me, and I want to explain—"

"I wanted to hear earlier. But that was earlier. I've realized it doesn't matter. It won't change anything."

"But won't you always wonder?" When he didn't answer she drew a shaky breath. "Sophie met him in Monaco, during her hen party. It was on the last night. I don't know all that happened, only that he was there, and then he wasn't."

"She went with him?"

She couldn't meet his eyes. "I didn't know then that she had. I thought she'd maybe gone to get air, or maybe popped up to the room to freshen her makeup. We waited for her in the casino. We were drinking bubbly and playing roulette and I kept looking for her as I'd saved her seat as it was next to mine."

"She didn't return."

"She was back in her bed when I woke up the next morning."

"But she wasn't there when you went to bed."

Poppy drew a deep breath. "No."

"What time was that?"

She hesitated, debating telling him the details, wondering whether or not the details mattered now, after everything else that had happened.

"Late."

"Midnight? One? Two?"

Later than that, she silently answered, seeing herself in the opulent hotel room, sitting in the upholstered chair closest to the door, holding her phone, keeping vigil.

The other girls had all gone to bed.

Poppy couldn't, imagining the worst. Poppy was just about to dress and go down to the hotel reception and ask if she should contact the police when the text arrived.

Am fine. With Renzo. Go to sleep.

After getting Sophie's text, Poppy pressed the phone to her brow and squeezed her eyes shut, heartsick instead of relieved.

The fact that Sophie knew she'd be worried was small comfort.

Everything had changed.

Poppy continued her vigil until four-thirty when she finally fell asleep in that overstuffed chair. She was still curled in the chair when she woke an hour later and discovered the room dark, and Sophie tucked into her bed, pretending to sleep.

"We never discussed it," Poppy said carefully, and that much was true. As they packed for their return to London, Sophie acted as if nothing had happened. And maybe nothing did happen. Maybe nothing would have happened. Maybe Sophie would have married Randall Grant this morning if Poppy hadn't sent the newspaper clippings to retired racecar driver, Renzo Crisanti, letting him know just who he'd taken to his bed five weeks before her wedding to the Earl of Langston.

On one hand, it was a terrible thing for Poppy to do.

On the other, it wouldn't have signified if Renzo hadn't stormed into the church and carried Sophie away with him.

Clearly, Sophie meant something to Renzo, and clearly Sophie had some interest in Renzo, too, because she hadn't kicked and screamed on the way out of the church.

It had been quite a scene, and profoundly uncomfortable, but the morning's events reassured Poppy that she'd done the right thing. She'd given Sophie not just a chance at love, but passion, too—

"Convenient," Dal said drily, sardonically. "Whatever you do, don't discuss the one thing that needs to be discussed."

The helicopter dipped and she grabbed at the harness straps connected to her lap belt and gave it a desperate tug. Thankfully, she was still secure, even though she felt as though her entire world had turned upside down.

Dal's gaze met hers, but he said nothing. He didn't need to, though. She could feel his fury.

Poppy looked away, out the window, fighting the emotion that threatened to overwhelm her as it crossed her mind that her note to Renzo hadn't just wrecked Sophie and Dal's wedding, but it'd wrecked her life, too.

Dal clenched his hand. He was so angry. So incredibly angry. He longed to smash his fist into Renzo Crisanti's face. He'd like to follow that blow with a series of hard jabs. Crisanti had no right. But then, Sophie had no right, either.

Jaw gritted, Dal glanced from the jagged red mountain range beneath them to Poppy's pale, stricken face and then he couldn't even look at her because she would marry him.

She didn't know it yet, but she didn't have a choice.

They traveled the rest of the way in tense silence, and then they were landing, heading for a sprawling pink villa. Tall, rose-pink walls surrounded the estate, while inside the walls it looked like a miniature kingdom complete with stables and barn, orchards and garden, and three different pools. They swooped lower, still, and her stomach dropped, too.

While the Gila airport transfer had been formal and choreographed, the arrival at the Kasbah was loud and joyous and chaotic. People were everywhere, and there was so much noise. Shouts and cheers and laughter and song.

Dal hadn't expected such a welcome, and from the look on Poppy's face, neither had she.

Poppy kept her smile fixed as she was greeted by one bowing, smiling woman after another, the women in long robes in bright jeweled colors. She was aware that the women greeted her only after first bowing to Randall. He, of course, received the biggest welcome, and it was a genuine welcoming, every staff member clearly delighted to see him. Several of the older men and women had tears in their eyes as they clasped his hand. One small, stooped woman kissed his hand repeatedly, tears falling.

Randall, so stoic in England, seemed to be fighting emotion as he leaned over to kiss the elderly woman's wrinkled cheek and murmur something in her ear.

Poppy got a lump in her throat as she looked at Randall with the tiny older woman. He wasn't affectionate with any of the staff in England, which made her even more curious about the elderly woman, but before she could ask, he brusquely explained the history as they walked toward the villa, shepherded by the jubilant staff.

"Izba was my mother's nanny," he said. "She used to look after me when we would visit Jolie. I hadn't expected her to still be alive."

"She was so emotional."

"She raised my mother from birth, and was closer to my mother than her own mother. Izba would have followed my mother to England, too, if my father had permitted it."

"Why wouldn't your father allow it?"

Randall shot her a mocking look. "He wanted my mother's wealth, not my mother's culture or family."

"It's not right to speak ill of the dead, but your father was—" She broke off, holding back the rest of the words.

"He was hard to love," Dal agreed. "And while he and I didn't have a good relationship, he was loving toward my brother. Andrew was his pride, his joy. My father was never the same after he died."

Poppy knew there had been a brother, but she'd never heard Randall speak of him, not in the four years she'd worked for Randall.

She shot him a troubled glance now, but before she could ask another question, they were climbing broad stairs and then passing beneath a graceful pink arch to enter a walled courtyard dominated by a huge blue fountain. White and purple bougainvillea covered the walls with pots of blooming lemon and orange trees in the corners of the courtyard. Two dark wooden doors were set in one of the long walls, and Randall opened one of those doors now.

"This is your suite," he said, leading her into a living room with a high ceiling covered in a dark carved wood. Windows lined one wall with the rest painted a warm golden khaki that made the floor-to-ceiling green-gold silk drapes shimmer in relief. The couch was covered in a vivid turquoise velvet; the two armchairs facing the sofa were covered in a luxurious silver silk. The lamps were silver, too, as was the giant sliding screen door that Randall pushed open to reveal the bedroom.

Again, one wall was nearly all floor-to-ceiling windows with views of the mountains and valley below. The bed dominated the large room, the bed itself enormous and low, covered in pristine white with two rows of plump white pillows. A long leather ottoman was placed at the foot of the bed while two silver nightstands were at the head of the bed. The ceiling had the same dark carved detail as in the living room, while a huge antique silver chandelier hung from the center of the ceiling, making the room glitter with soft iridescent light.

The space was expansive, furnishings were simple and yet the overall effect was sophisticated and glamorous. Poppy had slept in some beautiful rooms, but nothing came close to this understated luxury. Silks, satins and velvet. Furniture and wood covered in silver and gold.

"You're sure you want me in here? This looks like a room reserved for family."

"All rooms at the Kasbah are for family, and our special guests."

Something in his tone made her pulse jump. "When did I become a special guest?"

"When your job shifted from performing routine, mundane tasks to aiding me in a critical mission."

"Finding you a new secretary is a critical mission?"

"Absolutely. I'm a very busy, very important man. Surely you know that by now?" And then he smiled, his mocking, self-deprecating smile, and she felt a funny flutter in her chest. He was making fun of himself, teasing her in his self-deprecating manner, and she'd never been able to resist him when he made her smile.

"Can we please start with the search tomorrow? I'm beyond exhausted."

"Is this your way of saying you're not up for a big banquet tonight with live entertainment and a stream of visiting dignitaries?"

Poppy grimaced, unable to imagine a worse ending to what had been an absolutely horrendous day. "We're not really doing that, are we?"

"I am Prince Talal."

She saw the gleam in his golden eyes and the ache was back in her chest.

But then, she'd never been able to resist much about him. Even on the first day of work, she'd felt giddy in his presence. She'd thought that eventually she'd outgrow the juvenile reaction. Instead, she just developed deeper feelings, and a stronger attachment. "If you are indeed the prince, then you can excuse me from the lovely, but possibly lengthy, festivities."

"What if the festivities were short?"

"I've rather had it. I just want to go to bed and stay there forever."

"In that case, go to bed after dinner. Tomorrow is going to be a busy day. We have work to do, and since you're only here for fourteen days, we can't afford to waste any time."

"I'll be up early," she promised, unable to imagine life without him. It would be hard not seeing him almost every day. After she was gone, there would be no bounding out of bed, eager to get her day started.

"I'll have a tray sent to you," he said. "In the meantime, you'll find all the basics you'll need for the Kasbah in here." He opened one of the doors of the huge wardrobe. "I'm sure one of the dresses should fit, and then tomorrow one of the ladies' maids can adjust the others, and if need be, I can bring in a seamstress to make up anything else you might need."

"I don't need a lady's maid. I'm quite used to fending for myself."

"It would offend them if you refused assistance."

"Can you not explain that I'm English and eccentric?"

"Oh, I'm sure they'll realize just how eccentric you are, but please don't reject them. They've been trained by Izba, and Izba will want you happy."

Poppy sighed and rubbed at her forehead. "Fine. But there is no need to bring a seamstress in. I'm only here a short time and tunics are sort of a one-size-fits-all kind of dress. I should be fine without alterations."

"Sounds good. Sleep well, and I'll see you in the morning." Then he was gone, leaving her alone in the spacious suite.

Poppy had just opened the wardrobe to look for a nightgown when a light knock sounded on the door and then her door opened.

"Good evening," a young woman greeted Poppy in careful, stilted English. "May I please help you?"

"Thank you, but—" Poppy broke off, remembering Dal's warning and not wanting to offend anyone, much less within twenty minutes of arriving. "Yes, thank you. I was going to take a bath and then go to bed."

"I shall make your bath."

"Oh, no, I can start it myself. But I would like something for dinner. Perhaps salad or a sandwich?"

The young woman stared at Poppy clearly not understanding. "No bath?"

"Yes, I'll have a bath, but I can start it myself. I'd prefer if you could check on dinner."

"Please, more slowly." The girl's face crumpled. "My English is not so good."

So that was it. The poor girl didn't understand her. Poppy managed a tired smile. "Okay. Yes, I'll have a bath. Thank you."

Dal slept deeply, sleeping through the night and then until late in the morning, the blackout curtains in his room keeping the light out, allowing him to sleep far later than usual.

When he woke he was disoriented for a moment—the blackness of the room didn't help—and then it all came back to him.

The wedding.

The flight to Mehkar.

The helicopter ride to the Kasbah.

Dal left the bed and drew the heavy blackout curtains open, revealing brilliant sunshine. He could feel the heat trying to penetrate the thick glass windows. Thank goodness for thick stucco walls and triple glazed glass. The Kasbah remained cool even when temperatures soared outside.

He walked around his room, looking at it properly. This wasn't his room, at least, not the room he'd had as a boy. This room had been his grandfather's. It was the room reserved for the head of the family.

Apparently, here at Jolie he was the head of the family.

He felt like a disgrace.

He should have called his grandfather personally to let him know he was returning. He should have gone to the palace in Gila and met his grandfather for coffee or tea. He should have invited his grandfather here…

Dal opened the door to one of his terraces and stepped outside. Despite the heat, the air smelled fragrant, sweet.

He'd wondered if Jolie would still smell the same. It actually smelled better than he remembered—lavender and thyme, jasmine and orange blossoms.

He glanced down at the patio far below, and then at the tower off to his right. Past the tower he could see one of the tall external walls.

The Kasbah had been in the family hundreds of years, originally built as a fortress with thick external walls and tall towers offering vast, panoramic views ensuring that no one approached the Kasbah unseen.

The external walls were over fifteen feet tall and the same soft rose-peach hue as the palace itself, but once inside the huge gates, the hard surface of the walls disappeared, becoming a living garden, the plaster covered with flowering vines and lush scarlet, pink and white bougainvillea.

The Kasbah had been designed to protect the royal family in the event of a siege, with everything necessary for survival, but for a young boy that hadn't been its charm. Dal loved the towers and the secret rooms, the cool cellars and sunlit terraces with low couches piled high with silk pillows. He loved the clay pots used to cook his favorite dishes, chicken and lamb fragrant with saffron, fruit and spices.

The staff at Jolie was friendly, too, and in his mind, the staff had felt like family, always nodding and smiling and greeting him with warmth and pleasure.

Langston House was different. Even as a young boy he was aware of the difference and how no one smiled at Langston House. At Langston House the staff did not feel like family. They were servants. Menial. It was how his father liked things, the separation between classes, the distance between upstairs and downstairs. His father was the Fifth Earl of Langston, after all, raised with a clear sense of distinction and entitlement.

Dal's chest tightened up again, and he shifted in his seat, wishing he could just walk away from his past, and his father, but that would be the ultimate failure. His father had never expected Dal to succeed at anything, which is why Dal intended to keep his promise to his father—that he'd marry by thirty-five.

It was the only promise he'd ever made to his father and he'd honor the vow because then he'd be free.

And Dal longed to be free, not just of his father but the past.

With no time to waste, he rang for coffee and Poppy.

Poppy had thought her suite of rooms was lovely, but they were nothing compared to Dal's magnificent suite, which literally took up the entire second floor of the villa, bordered on all sides by sundrenched terraces and patios and fragrant, private gardens.

Like her, he had a living room and bedroom suite,

but he also had a dining room, and office, all four rooms with the same floor-to-ceiling windows and doors that filled her suite with light.

He had papers, a notebook, pen and computer on a table outside, the area shaded by an elegant pergola covered with blooming jasmine.

"Is it too warm for you out here?" he asked, gesturing for her to sit in the chair by the laptop.

"It's comfortable now," she said, "but it'll definitely be quite hot later."

"I promise we'll move inside to an air-conditioned room before you melt."

She sat down in the low wooden chair with the teal pillows. "What am I to call you here? Dal? Prince Talal? Izba referred to you as Sheikh Talal, as well as His Highness. You have so many names."

"Not that many. My staff at the Kasbah will either call me Prince Talal, or Sheikh Talal. My family in Mehkar calls me Tal, although when we were in Gila, at the airport, my cousin addressed me as His Highness due to protocol."

"Your cousin? Which one was he?"

"The last man on the carpet."

"The one you hugged."

"Yes." Randall's mouth curved but his eyes were shuttered. "The last time I saw him he was just six years old. Now he's a man."

"How old were you the last time you were here?"

"Ten."

"You've both grown up."

"We have," he said, but there was no joy in his voice, just loss, and regret. And then his broad shoulders squared and his voice firmed. "Now to your question, you may call me anything you want, provided it's not Randall."

"You dislike your proper name that much?"

"My father is the only other person who has ever called me Randall."

She felt a shiver of distaste. No wonder he didn't like it. "I wish you'd told me that earlier."

"I tried. But you insisted Dal was too personal."

"I'm sorry."

"It's fine. Clearly, I survived the horror."

She shot him a swift look and was relieved to see that faint ironic smile of his. A smile she was learning that he used to hide hurts and needs, and all those emotions he viewed as weak. "But this is exactly what I mean. You have to talk. Tell people things. If I knew that the only other person who called you Randall was your father, and your father and you were not close, and it wasn't a positive or comfortable association—"

"You're getting a little carried away. You haven't inflicted any damage. I'm no more scarred than when you first met me."

She must have looked sufficiently startled because he grimaced. "That was supposed to make you smile."

Her brows pulled. "Do you think you're very scarred?"

"I was being amusing. Don't read too much into it."

But she couldn't help reading into it. She'd heard some horror stories about Randall's father, the Fifth Earl of Langston, and she'd long suspected that Dal's isolated nature was due to his father's volatility. Poppy carefully chose her next words. "Were you close to your mother?"

"Yes."

"What did she call you?"

"Tal."

All these years she'd thought she'd known him. She'd prided herself on knowing him better than anyone, but as it turned out, she didn't know the real Dal Grant at all. "Who are you?" she asked, smiling unsteadily.

His smile faded and he glanced away for a moment and when he looked back at her, his expression struck her as rather bleak. "Interesting question, Miss Marr. I'll have to get back to you on that one."

And then just as quickly, the darkness was gone and he was back to business. "Let's get started, shall we? I know you follow all of Sophie's friends, so how about we start by pulling up Seraphina's Instagram page—"

"No."

"No?"

"I'm not going to pore over Seraphina's social media. Or Florrie's. I promised I'd help find a new secretary, not a replacement for Sophie."

"I'd like your input on both."

"This makes me uncomfortable."

"It should. If you hadn't interfered yesterday, I'd be a married man today."

"You just think I did something, but you have no proof."

"And when I have proof? What then? How will you make it up to me?"

She shook her head, lips compressed.

"Poppy, I made my father a promise, and I'm not going to break that promise."

"Then perhaps you need a better list," she said, picturing Seraphina and Florrie. Both had been at

Langston House yesterday for the wedding. Florrie was single at the moment—in between polo player lovers—and Seraphina was dating someone. It was in the early stages of the relationship but she apparently liked him and had told everyone he could be the one. Although that wasn't the first, or second, or even third time she'd said such a thing. "Only Florrie is currently single. Seraphina is seeing someone. She brought him to the wedding yesterday."

"I didn't notice."

"I'm not surprised. It was a tad hectic." She studied Dal, who looked handsome and rested this morning, his crisp white linen shirt the perfect foil for his black hair and golden eyes. "So tell me, how do you intend to proceed with your wooing?"

"I'll make a phone call, explain that I'm in need of a countess, and ask if she's interested."

"That's it?"

"Should I ask her to fill out an application and give five references?"

"Dal, this isn't the way to a satisfying relationship."

"You're a relationship expert now?"

She ignored the jab. "I'm not the one rushing into marriage, and I know it's been difficult these past few days, but you can't truly want a shallow, materialistic woman who is only marrying you for the title and money?"

"But that's exactly what I'm offering, and all I'm really offering—"

"That is not so. She gets you. *You.* And yes, you're a horrible, ridiculous, stubborn, awful man, but you're still you. Why give yourself to someone who doesn't care about you?"

"Because she'll be happier with the title and houses and bank account than she will with me."

"I don't know why you're saying these things."

"Why not let her enjoy herself? As long as she gives me heirs, she can do what she wants."

"I don't want to hear any more."

"It shouldn't upset you. You crossed yourself off the list of candidates. Who I marry, or how I choose my wife, shouldn't trouble you in the least."

"But of course it does! I care about you. I care about your happiness, or lack of happiness. I care that you lock yourself away from the world and just work, work, work. I care that you lost Sophie, and now you're in this position, but at the same time, I'm glad you didn't trap Sophie in a cold marriage. That wouldn't have been fair to her. She deserves so much more. And you deserve more, too, but you won't demand more and that absolutely baffles me."

She lifted the computer, rose and walked away.

Dal didn't stop her, letting her march away with the laptop as if she was the injured party.

She wasn't injured. She was lucky. She would soon have everything she wanted, and more.

A husband, a family, financial security, as well as respect. Once she was his wife, she'd have power and prestige. People would fall all over themselves wanting her approval, trying to ingratiate themselves.

She would be fine. He, on the other hand, was not. Normally, he was quite good at compartmentalizing emotions and suppressing anger, but he felt barely in control at the moment. He was being tested as his past, present and future collided together in a sickening crash of memories and emotions.

When he'd pictured Kasbah Jolie yesterday, he'd pictured a remote estate, someplace peaceful, and he'd imagined he'd arrive with very little fanfare, but the transfer in Gila had been anything but understated. The royal carpet, the line of dignitaries, the military guard behind, the royal helicopter itself. He hadn't wanted any of it. His flight crew had contacted the executive terminal at Gila and arranged for a helicopter for the Earl of Langston, but at no time had they dropped his Mehkar title. They couldn't have, as they didn't know it.

Which meant someone at the Gila airport had contacted the palace, and the king had ordered the welcome.

Dal frowned, his chest as heavy as his gut.

His grandfather knew he was here, aware that Dal had not just come home, but had once again shut him out, choosing to retreat to the mountain palace rather than attempt any form of reconciliation.

Dal didn't know why he was treating his grandfather the same way his father had—with callous contempt and utter disregard. What was wrong with him? Why couldn't he be kind to the one man who'd always been kind to him?

Dal planned on accomplishing two things before he left Mehkar: he'd be married, and he'd finally make peace with his grandfather.

CHAPTER SIX

POPPY SETTLED DOWN to work at the desk in the library on the main floor. The room had a soaring, dark-beamed ceiling, arched windows and walls the color of deep red rubies. The beamed ceiling had been stenciled in gold, and the big light fixtures were gold, and then there were the floor-to-ceiling shelves filled with leather-bound books that looked to be hundreds of years old.

Poppy had discovered the room earlier this morning and couldn't wait to return. She opened her laptop, checked the internet and was pleased to see that it worked just as well here as it did at home. It wasn't long before she had accessed all her files through the cloud storage system on the laptop. All of Dal's companies used the same cloud storage, making it easy to use any computer, anywhere.

She checked her email, and then scanned BBC's news and then reached out by email to several prominent employment agencies, sharing the details about the secretarial position to be filled, and how they were hoping to fill the job as soon as possible.

She received a reply from each almost immediately. One wanted her to fill out a more complete questionnaire, while the other promised to begin forwarding résumés later that afternoon.

With no résumés to review yet, Poppy wasn't quite sure what to do with her time next.

And then she thought of Sophie. Where was she? And how was she?

Poppy opened her email and sent Sophie a quick message.

I'm with Dal in Mehkar. Where are you? How are you? Fill me in, please!

And then, because her curiosity was getting the best of her, she went back online and studied Florrie and Seraphina's social media accounts.

Florrie had shared a photograph taken outside Langston House before the wedding had begun. She was with Seraphina and several other beautiful girls and they were all smiling for the camera.

Seraphina was a dark brunette and Florrie was a golden blonde. They were both gorgeous and glamorous, and they knew how to wear clothes well.

But that didn't make them good matches for Dal.

Poppy was staring at the photo hard, so hard, she didn't hear Dal enter the library.

"Are you trying to decide which one is better for me?" he asked, leaning over her desk chair to get a better look at the photo of four smiling women.

She closed the computer quickly. "What are you doing here?"

"Checking on your progress. Any good résumés yet?"

"One agency asked me to fill out a questionnaire,

while the other has promised to begin forwarding résumés straightaway."

"Was the questionnaire complicated?"

"No." She wiggled in her chair, not willing to admit that she'd somehow managed to forget all about completing the form. She didn't know how she could forget.

"So you are all done with everything right now?"

"I'm caught up for the moment, if that's what you're asking."

"Yes. Great. I'd like your help in my search." He lifted a hand to stop her when she started to protest. "And I know you don't want to. Sophie was your friend and you're very loyal to her, but Sophie is no longer in the picture and I need a wife."

"But how can I help you when you won't even help yourself?"

"What does that mean?"

"You can't treat your next fiancé the way you treated Sophie. It was criminal. You were the King of Cold, the Master of Remote." She shrugged at his frown. "It's true, Dal. I'm telling you the truth. Please don't propose to another woman without being willing to give her more."

Dal couldn't believe they were back to discussing this intangible "more" again. It was beyond infuriating.

It was also beyond infuriating to have to play this game with her. He wasn't even considering Florrie or Seraphina as a future wife. There was only one woman on his list and that was Poppy. But if he told Poppy that, she'd have a nervous breakdown, and they didn't need that. He had to get married, but he preferred marrying someone stable. And most days Poppy was stable. She was also dependable, and someone he trusted. Perhaps Sophie had done him a huge favor.

"I'm not sure I know how to go about demanding more," he said flatly, battling to hide his irritation. "I am not sure I even know what this 'more' would look like."

"More is just more, Dal. More companionship. More conversation. More laughter. Possibly more tears—"

"Not that, please."

She sighed, but continued on. "More would also be more friendship, and more support, more encouragement, more happiness."

"That's a great deal of more."

"Yes, it requires some thought and effort, but that's how you develop a relationship. It's how people get to know you, and you would get to know them. It takes time, too." Her wide brown eyes met his. "And it's not something money can buy. So you can't throw money at it. If anything, money makes it worse."

"How so?"

Her brows pulled, her expression troubled. "Money is power, and power thrives on inequality. True friendship, just like true love, doesn't care about position, or prestige. It wants what is best for the other person."

Her words grated on his nerves, putting an uncomfortable knot in his chest. He didn't know why her thoughts bothered him so much, but it took every bit of his control not to retort sharply, mockingly. He didn't like the world of feelings and emotions. He didn't enjoy the company of emotional people. Poppy was the sole exception, and maybe that was because at work he could normally steer her in a different direction, and she'd oblige him. But here, here was proving to be a different matter.

"Please don't make me lose all respect for you," he said with a hard, sardonic smile. "Feelings are massively overrated."

"But I didn't specifically say *feelings*," she answered quietly. "I was very careful not to use the word *feelings*. Apparently, that's all you heard, though."

"I think I stopped listening when you said I couldn't solve the problem by throwing money at it."

"You can make all the jokes you want, but you can't change the truth, and the truth is, you have to open up more, and give more and be present in the lives of those who love you."

He shot her a wry glance. "You make me sound like an ass."

"Well, you can be intolerable at times."

"And yet you're still fighting to save me."

"Just for another two weeks."

"So altruistic, then, trying to whip me into shape for the next secretary."

"I'm more concerned about the next fiancée. She's the one that would get the short end of the stick because she will expect a relationship. The secretary won't."

"Have you always been so pragmatic?"

"Charity girls can't afford to wear rose-colored glasses."

And yet Poppy did. Poppy was the least practical, most idealistic woman he'd ever met. He functioned best when his world was cool, precise and analytical… the complete opposite of the world Poppy inhabited.

"Perhaps you didn't get the memo," he answered, aware that she'd had a difficult past. Poppy had lost her mother to cancer and then her father died ten years later, leaving Poppy all alone. Or, she would have been alone if it wasn't for Sophie. "You love your fairy tales and rainbows."

"You forgot lemon drops and fireworks. I love those, too." Then she shrugged. "I know it's hard for you to stomach, but my parents met in school, fell in love and never dated anyone else. They were totally devoted to each other, as well as really happy together…despite Mum's cancer, and the creditors constantly calling."

Her shoulders shifted. "And then when they were both gone, Sophie gave me a second home. She looked after me and showed me what real friendship is. I learned that love isn't just a romantic thing. Love is kindness and commitment and doing what's best for the other person. And that's what I want for you. I want you to have a kind wife. A woman who will commit to you and do what's best for you, and in return, you would be kind to her, and loyal to her and put her needs first, too."

"If you care so much about my happiness, why not just marry me? Wouldn't that be the simplest thing to do?"

For a long moment she said nothing, and then her throat worked and her voice sounded low and rough. "I've never had much in life in terms of material things, but I was loved, dearly, by my parents, and if I ever marry, it will be for love. A marriage without love is doomed from the start."

By the time Poppy made it back to her room, she was absolutely worn out.

These intense conversations with Dal drained her, and part of her wanted to just give up on him and stop trying to help, but the only way she could handle the idea of leaving him was by thinking she was leaving him better off than he was now.

The man didn't need more money. The man didn't need more people to bow and scrape. What Dal needed was honesty. He needed someone to care enough about him to tell him the truth. He needed to be pushed to try harder and give more and be more…and she knew he could, because during the past four years she'd seen a softer side of him. She'd experienced his kindness and patience firsthand. He knew how to talk and be good company, too. But she also knew that it had to be his choice, on his terms, or he'd just shut you out and become that remote, unfeeling ice man that Sophie dreaded.

Poppy showered and then wrapped a cotton robe around her and headed to the wardrobe to see what she'd wear for dinner.

Poppy knew from this morning that the wardrobe was full of long tunics in every color of the rainbow. She'd stroked the vivid fabrics, pausing at a brilliant green gown with gold embellishments from the plunging neckline all the way down the gauzy fabric, and then an ivory one, and another ivory one this time with hot pink fringe all around the sleeves and edges of the long, narrow skirt. The dresses were like art, each unique but stylish and impossibly pretty. Poppy didn't know how she was supposed to choose just one to wear when they were all so beautiful.

She now flipped through all the dresses again, this time stopping at a rich gold dress with full three-quarter sleeves. The sleeves were dotted with a graphic black-and-white sunburst pattern, with black-and-white trim down the front, and along the hem of the straight gold skirt.

But Poppy's favorite part of the dress were the two playful black-and-white fringe pom-poms that hung from the V-neckline.

"Would be beautiful on you, my lady," a soft voice said from behind her in slow, broken English.

Poppy turned around and smiled as she spotted Izba in the doorway.

"These gowns are exquisite," Poppy said.

Izba stepped into the room and closed the door behind her. "His Highness Talal's mother designed them," she said, crossing to the wardrobe and reaching into the closet to draw out a white lace kaftan with coral-red embroidery on the shoulders and vibrant coral-red fringe at the sleeves and hem. "She thought clothes should make a woman happy."

Izba spoke with a quiet sincerity that put a lump in Poppy's throat. "Talal's mother was very talented," Poppy answered huskily.

The elderly woman's dark brown eyes shone and she carefully hung the white lace gown up. "She was most beautiful woman in Mehkar, but with the most beautiful heart in the world." She turned around to look at Poppy. "Which dress you wish to wear for tonight?"

"I don't know which one to pick. What do you think I should wear?"

Izba's lips pursed and her dark gaze swept Poppy before she faced the closet again. She studied the rack for a long moment, cheeks puffing, until she reached in and lifted out a dark cherry gown with big cheerful silver flowers embroidered across the bodice before becoming delicate trailing flowers down the skirt.

The sleeves were plain except for a thick silver bank
of embroidery at the cuff.

"These are poppies," Izba said in her careful, stilted
English. "Just like your name, yes?"

Poppy didn't know why she wanted to cry. Instead,
she nodded and smiled. "That's perfect."

"Perfect," Izba echoed carefully, smiling affection-
ately. "Once you are dressed, I will fix your hair."

"Oh, I don't need help with my hair."

"His Highness expects us to help you."

"Yes, but his—" Poppy broke off, unable to call
Randall anything remotely like His Highness, and she
searched for the right words. "His…your Prince Talal…
knows I am accustomed to taking care of myself. I prefer taking care of myself."

Izba's already wrinkled brow creased further. "But
as his wife—"

"Oh! No. *No.* I think there's been a mistake, and I
understand the confusion, but I'm not his wife. I work
for Talal. I'm his secretary."

Izba stared at her, dark eyes assessing. "You are not
just friend. You are to marry the prince."

"No! Oh, Izba, no." Poppy swallowed hard, thinking this was incredibly uncomfortable but she had to
make the older woman understand. "Believe me, I am
not marrying Prince Talal. I serve as his secretary,
nothing more." She drew a quick breath. "I've agreed
to help him find a wife, but Izba, it's not me."

Before they came to Jolie, Dal would have described
Poppy as pretty, in a fresh, wholesome, no-nonsense
sort of way with her thick, shoulder-length brown hair
and large, brown eyes and a serious little chin.

But as Poppy entered the dining room with its glossy

white ceiling and dark purple walls, she looked anything but wholesome and no-nonsense.

She was wearing a silk gown the color of cherries, delicately embroidered with silver threads, and instead of her usual ponytail or chignon, her dark hair was down, and long, elegant chandelier earrings dangled from her ears. As she walked, the semi-sheer kaftan molded to her curves, highlighting her full, firm breasts and swell of hips.

"It seems I've been keeping you waiting," she said, her voice pitched lower than usual and slightly breathless. "Izba insisted on all this," she added, gesturing up toward her face.

At first Dal thought she was referring to the ornate silver earrings that were catching and reflecting the light, but once she was seated across from him he realized her eyes had been rimmed with kohl and her lips had been outlined and filled in with a soft plum-pink gloss. "You're wearing makeup."

"Quite a lot of it, too." She grimaced. "I tried to explain to Izba that this wasn't me, but she's very determined once she makes her mind up about something and apparently, dinner with you requires me to look like a tart."

Dal checked his smile. "You don't look like a tart. Unless it's the kind of tart one wants to eat."

Color flooded Poppy's cheeks and she glanced away, suddenly shy, and he didn't know if it was her shyness or the shimmering dress that clung to her curves, outlining her high, full breasts, but he didn't think any woman could be more beautiful, or desirable than Poppy right now. "You look lovely," he said quietly. "But I don't want you uncomfortable all through din-

ner. If you'd rather go remove the makeup I'm happy
to wait."

She looked at him closely as if doubting his sincerity. "It's fun to dress up, but I'm worried Izba has the
wrong idea about me."

"And what is that?"

"She seems to think you're going to…marry…me."

When he said nothing, she added, "I know I'm not
on your 'list' anymore, and so I'm not suggesting you're
encouraging her, but it's awkward trying to convince
her that I'm not going to be your new wife."

"I'll have a word with her," he said, and he would
have a word with Izba, but not about this. The fact was,
Poppy would be his wife. She was going to marry him.
He knew exactly how to get her acquiescence. Women
thought they needed words. But even more than language, they needed touch.

He was trying to hold off on seduction, though. He
didn't want to trick her into being his wife, nor did he
want to use her body against her. But she would ca-
pitulate, if he seduced her. She was already his even
without a single touch.

His goal was to get her to think marriage was her
idea. It was far better to let her believe the idea was
hers. She'd be a far happier, and more malleable bride
that way.

"Thank you." She glanced down, fingertips grazing
the silver beadwork near her shoulder. "Did you know
this is your mother's design?"

"What do you mean?"

"Every dress in the wardrobe in my room was designed by your mother. Izba said she was an aspiring
fashion designer when she married your father."

"I didn't know," he said after a long moment. "I had no idea." He frowned at the candle on the table, surprised that such a little detail should knock him off guard, but it did. It might be a small thing, but it said so much about who she was, and the dreams she'd had.

"She had tremendous style," he said gruffly. "I always knew she was different from other mums, but I don't think I appreciated the differences until it was too late."

"I wish I'd had the chance to meet her. She sounds so lovely."

"She was." And then because he found the memories unbearable, he smashed the past, making the memories vanish. As the memories faded, so did the ache. The ache didn't completely disappear, but at least it was manageable.

He signaled to one of the stewards standing in the corner. "Let's eat."

Dinner was a feast, with salad after salad, followed by warm, fragrant pilaf and delicious pan-seared salmon, and of course there was dessert, the waiter tempting Poppy with the description of the honey and mint syrup cake served with a small scoop of spiced vanilla ice cream on the side.

Poppy was full from dinner and was going to reluctantly pass on the cake, until Dal suggested she skip the ice cream and try a slice. He said the cake had just been baked; he'd smelled it earlier in the oven and it was his favorite cake because it was topped with a thick, crunchy layer of slivered honey-glazed almonds.

Poppy couldn't resist the description and the cake was even better than Dal described. She ate her slice, and had just popped a stray slivered almond into her mouth when Dal leaned back in his chair and told her he'd spoken with Seraphina earlier.

Poppy almost choked on the almond. She coughed to clear her throat. "You called her?"

"I did," he said casually as if this was no big deal.

"When?"

"This afternoon." His broad shoulders shifted carelessly. "She was surprised to hear from me, but she quickly warmed up. It seems she and her new boyfriend had a fight on the drive home from the wedding." He looked at her, lashes lowering, concealing the gold of his eyes. "She's not sure if it's going to work out between them."

Poppy's heart fell. She didn't know why she felt such a rush of disappointment. She should want this for him. He needed a wife. Quickly. If tall, slim, Sloane Ranger Seraphina could fit the bill, why shouldn't he marry her?

"That's good," she said faintly, struggling to smile. Many would consider Seraphina an excellent substitution for Sophie. Seraphina's family was far wealthier than the Carmichael-Joneses, and Seraphina was wildly popular, always in the press, photographed at all the right events, and big parties and fashion shows.

The fact that she was as shallow as a plate was only problematic if one wanted a wife with emotions…

"You don't sound very convincing," he said, reaching for his wineglass. "I thought you'd be pleased. I'd much rather narrow down my list to just one and focus on courting her, rather than jumping back and forth between two women."

"You don't want to even give Florrie a chance?"

"I was under the impression that you didn't think Florrie would be a suitable match."

"I never said anything against her."

"But you implied she's one of those horsey girls, always at a polo match."

"Did I? I don't remember."

"I ride, but I'm not by any means an equestrian. If polo is her passion, she wouldn't be happy with me."

"And Seraphina is a clothes horse, always seen in the front row of some fashion show or other."

"Yes, but I wouldn't be expected to attend the fashion shows with her. That's something she could do on her own, and no one would think twice about her being in Paris or Milan or New York without me."

"Don't you want to be with your wife?"

"No."

"Dal!"

"Don't you want your wife to want to be with you?"

"Not really. I enjoy my own company. Besides, if Seraphina is currently disgruntled with the new boyfriend, she'll welcome my attention and it shouldn't take much effort to close the deal with her."

"I've never heard a worse proposal."

"I'm not a romantic man."

"That might be why you lost Sophie."

He gave her a look that wasn't pleasant. Clearly, he didn't appreciate her honesty, but honesty is what he needed. "Women aren't things to park on shelves or in closets. They want and need time and attention."

"The *more* you're constantly harping on."

"Or in your case, some. *Some* time. *Some* attention." She was angry now, and she didn't even try to hide her irritation. "Never mind a token of affection, because I know you gave Sophie almost none."

"Sophie didn't like being touched."

"Sophie *craved* affection. You're the one that rejected her."

"She recoiled every time I reached for her."

"But did you talk to her before you reached for her? Did you take her to dinner? Did you send her flowers? Did you plan anything fun? No. It was strictly business, and cold as hell."

"And you've thought this all these years?"

"Yes."

"Why didn't you say something?"

"Because it wasn't my place, and she didn't complain, not until this last year, and then she wasn't complaining as much as...panicking. I thought maybe the sheer size of the wedding was overwhelming her, but clearly it wasn't the wedding. It was you."

"Of course you'll be Team Sophie until the bitter end."

"I'm on your team, too. That's why I'm spoiling my delicious dessert, trying to make you understand that it takes two to make a marriage. You can't just put a ring on someone's finger and be done with it."

"I did care about Sophie. I cared a great deal. But the fact is, I couldn't seem to make her happy. It was as if she didn't want to be happy with me—"

"You're just saying that now."

"You wanted honesty. I'm being honest. She didn't want to marry me. But she couldn't stand up to her parents."

"And when did you realize this? Five and a half years ago?"

"No. This past year. I tried to plan several special

occasions for us—theater, shopping, dinner. She agreed to each and looked beautiful every time we stepped out, but there was no…conversation. There was no… warmth. Even her smiles looked forced as if she was suffering and barely tolerating my company."

"Martyred for the cause," Poppy muttered.

Dal glanced at her, eyes narrowed. "What did you say?"

She was so annoyed with him, and all of them. Money and power changed people, inflating their sense of worth, and bringing out the worst in them. "Your fathers shouldn't have arranged the marriage, not against your wishes."

"I didn't protest very much. It was easier just to make him happy. Less conflict, and honestly, I didn't care who I married."

"Why not?"

"I don't feel emotions like you. I don't feel love, and I wouldn't have ever married for love."

"Well, Sophie did, and she tried to fight it." Poppy saw Dal's startled expression. "I overheard them once, Sophie and her parents. It was a terrible row. They said terrible things to her, squashing her completely." She swallowed hard. "I think that's why she stuck up for me, from early on. Because she never had anyone who stuck up for her."

And this was why Poppy did what she did, sending newspaper clippings to Renzo Crisanti.

She wanted Sophie to have a chance at happiness. She wanted Sophie to have more.

Just as she still wanted Dal to have more.

"You're making me feel like the devil," Dal said roughly.

"That's not my intention."

He shifted at the table, features tight, jaw jutting. "I had no idea she'd been pressured to marry me. It disgusts me to think that she was being forced into a marriage with me."

"You both deserved better."

He rose from the table and crossed the room, hands in his trouser pockets. "No wonder you looked elated when Crisanti showed up. You were thrilled she'd escaped the marriage. You were thrilled she was escaping marrying me."

"Yes," she answered. "I was. No woman should be forced into marriage with a man. Not even if it's in marriage to you."

"Thanks…?"

"You know I mean it in the nicest, sincerest way, because you're aware of how I feel about you. I have that…soft spot. I see all the good things in you that Sophie couldn't see."

"Really? What did you fall in love with, since it clearly wasn't my title and wealth?"

"You give to others, constantly, generously. You provide leadership to developing countries. You donate money to developing businesses, particularly businesses headed by women. But you don't just give money, you give time, and wisdom, and you listen to these people. You truly care."

"So why did you take yourself off my list?"

"Because you care about everyone but yourself. You don't love yourself. You barely like yourself, and it would be difficult, if not impossible, being your wife when I know you'd never love me—"

"But I'd want you."

"Not the same thing."

"Physical pleasure can be incredibly satisfying."

"But it's not love, and I want true love, and I'm holding out for a man who will move the moon and stars for me."

He made a rough, mocking sound. "I understand that I expect too little from marriage, but you, my darling Poppy, expect too much."

"Maybe. But I'd rather believe in happy-ever-after then be bitter, cold and cynical."

"Like me?"

"I think you're cynical because it's easier than trying to muddle through with emotions. Far better to be coldly intellectual than a flesh and blood human being—"

"Just because I don't believe in romantic love doesn't mean I don't bleed when cut."

"I've never seen you bleed, or grieve. You lost your fiancée yesterday and yet you never shed a tear."

"Maybe because she wasn't the right one for me. Maybe because I'm relieved that I have an unexpected opportunity to find the right woman and make this work."

"You're not acquiring a company, Dal. You're talking about marrying a woman!"

"And I think you're angry because you'd like to be that woman, only you're too afraid to allow your dreams to become reality—"

"A life with you isn't my dream. You would never, ever be able to give me what I need!"

He crossed the room, walking toward her with such deliberate intention that it made her heart race. "That's just another excuse. You are full of them today. Why don't you stop acting like a little girl and fight for what you want?"

She backed up a panicked step. "You're not what I want!"

"Bullshit." And then he trapped her against the wall, wrapped an arm low around her waist and pulled her close.

Poppy knew a split second before his head dropped that he was going to kiss her, and she stiffened, shocked, surprised, but also curious.

And then his mouth covered hers and she felt an electric jolt shoot through her. He was right about her fantasies. She'd imagined this for years. She'd had a few dates here and there but she was essentially an inexperienced, twenty-six-year-old virgin. It had been easy remaining a virgin, too, because Dal was the only man she wanted, and how could any other man measure up to him? No one was as handsome. No one as intelligent. No one as powerful.

And now he was holding her, kissing her and tremor after tremor coursed through her. The kiss felt like a claiming. There was nothing tentative in the way his mouth slanted over hers, his mouth warm, his breath cool. Her senses felt flooded and her brain struggled to take it all in…his smell, his warmth and then there was that delicious pressure of his body so hard and lean against her, his chest a wall of muscles.

His head finally lifted and he stared deep into her eyes. "Tell me you didn't want that to happen."

"Do you enjoy humiliating women?"

"I wanted it to happen." His narrowed gaze examined every inch of her face. "Because I've spent years trying not to imagine that kiss."

* * *

It was true, too. Dal would have never kissed her while engaged, or married. He would have never acted on any kind of impulse—there would be no impulse—if he wasn't single, but he was single now and she was single, and she was more than available. When she looked at him, she practically offered herself up to him. The sacrificial maiden, the innocent virgin—

He stopped himself, brow furrowing as he glanced at her. "Are you a virgin?"

Her cheeks burned with color. Her eyes flashed dangerously. "That is none of your business."

"So it's a yes," he answered, fascinated by the bloom in her cheeks and the bruised pink of her lips. Emotion darkened her eyes now, making her wonder what she'd look like after she'd shattered with pleasure.

"There is no need for you to be horrible," she protested breathlessly.

She was aroused but fighting it.

He respected her more for fighting it. "Not trying to be horrible," he said, thinking she needed another kiss, as did he. "Just trying to figure out why you still want to fight the attraction. There's no reason. Sophie is gone. I'm single. You're single."

"You are so incredibly unromantic."

"Lust isn't always romantic, but it's real."

"Well, I don't lust for you. I have feelings for you. A huge difference."

"But that's where you're wrong. You might have feelings for me, but you also desire me. I can prove it."

Her eyes had clung to his as he spoke, her wide, dark eyes showing every single thing she was feeling. She was aroused and curious but also remarkably shy and innocent. Holding her against him, he could feel how her slim body hummed with tension, as well as the wild beating of her heart. She was as soft as he was hard, as warm as he was cold, and as he gazed down into her lovely expressive eyes, he thought Sophie had indeed done him a favor.

Dal could imagine Poppy as his wife. A sweet, kind, warm wife. The kind of woman who'd be a sweet, kind, warm mother, too.

"Let's revisit the subject of lust," he said, just before his head dipped and his mouth covered hers to part her full, soft lips and plunder the inside of her hot, sweet mouth. His tongue teased hers, stirring her senses, making her clutch at his arms and whimper against his mouth.

He pressed her closer, shaping her to him, his hand settling on her pert, round derriere. He cupped her bottom, caressing the generous curve, and she shuddered and arched against him, her entire body trembling as if he'd set her on fire.

He shifted around so that he could lean back against the wall while he positioned her between his thighs. He felt hard and savage as he drew her hips against his hips, letting her feel the heavy length of his erection.

She sighed against his mouth, and her breasts peaked against his chest. He relished the feel of her tight nipples and he stroked up, from her hips over the small of her waist to caress the side of her full breast.

She shivered again and made soft, incoherent sounds that heated his blood and made him want to rip her dress off and devour her here.

It had been so long since he'd been with anyone, and

forever since he'd felt this way. He'd forgotten what desire felt like. He'd forgotten the insistent throb of need, and the need to claim. And he didn't want just anyone, he wanted her, all of her, and the more she gave, the more he wanted to take. His thumb found her breast, her nipple pebbled tight, pressing through the thin silk of her kaftan. He rubbed the tip, pinching it, just to hear her gasp and feel her hips twist against his.

He ached, and his erection throbbed and he felt more alive than he had in years. Not just years. But decades.

He stroked Poppy's full, round breast again, and beneath her breast, before palming the fullness, savoring the shape and weight. He loved her curves, and her sensual nature, amazed that she'd hidden both all these years with her ugly practical wardrobe and shy, retiring smile.

Poppy was not shy or retiring at all.

Poppy was a goddess and he could not wait to take her to bed.

She was exactly what he needed. And he would have her. It wasn't a matter of if, but when.

Reluctantly, he lifted his head. Her dark eyes were cloudy and her gaze unfocused. She swayed in his arms, off balance.

"We'll marry end of this week," he said tightly, reining in his hunger so that he could attempt to be logical and rational. "I don't know if you want to stay here for a honeymoon, or if you'd want to travel somewhere else."

She blinked up at him, still dazed. *"What?"*

"It will just be a very simple ceremony. A civil ceremony. And then with formalities done, we can do what we want. Honeymoon here, or travel to someplace you've never been."

She gave him a shove, freeing herself. "I'm not marrying you!"

"You are, and you want to. Stop fighting the inevitable."

Her face flushed pink. "Excuse me, but what planet are you living on? I never agreed to marry you, and just because I kissed you doesn't mean we're suddenly a couple."

"We should be."

"Because I kissed you back? Ha!" She took another quick step back, arms folding over her chest. "I have kissed dozens of men and I've never married any of them!"

"I don't care if you kissed three hundred. You're a virgin. You want me. You belong to me."

"Ahem. I don't belong to you, or with you. In fact, I gave notice that I'm leaving you. So, maybe you need to go out there and find someone you can actually date, and court and hopefully marry before you lose your precious earldom and your historic Langston House!"

Poppy practically fled back to her room, nearly bumping into Imma as she threw open her door.

Poppy wished Imma a good night and then once alone, began to pace her floor before flinging herself on her bed, replaying the entire scene with Dal in her head. What a scene it was! The words he'd said, those obnoxious, arrogant words, and then the kiss…

Oh, the kiss…

But no, she wouldn't think about the kiss. That was the most impossible thing of all, too much like the fairy tales she'd loved as a girl because those stories about good and evil, lightness and darkness, helped explain the world and the things that had happened in her world—the financial struggles, her mother's prolonged battle with cancer, a battle they'd thought she'd won, *twice*, only to relapse and die just after Poppy's thirteenth birthday. It had just gotten worse after that. Her father couldn't juggle his job and fatherhood and on the advice of friends, had found a boarding school that offered scholarships to promising young women in need.

She was in need, but poverty was the least of her woes.

She missed her mother and her father and what she'd thought of as family.

But just when she didn't think she could take any more, there was Sophie, lovely, strong Sophie, who took Poppy under her wing, becoming her champion when Poppy was at her lowest.

Sophie had given Poppy her hope back, and hope was everything. Hope made one look forward. Hope helped one to focus on what lay ahead rather than what was behind. Hope made all things possible, and had more than once lifted her from despair.

Hope also meant that she could dream of happy endings, if not for her, then for Sophie, which is why Poppy had written to Renzo in the first place. Poppy had wanted to save Sophie from a loveless marriage. She wanted Sophie to have the life she deserved, which meant true love. Passionate love. Forever love.

The kind of love Poppy's parents had. Poppy's father had dearly loved her mother, taking her to every chemo and radiation treatment and staying with her after.

His love had been fierce and unwavering even to the bitter end.

The love and tenderness he'd shown her mother allowed her mother to say, even after she'd been taken to hospice, that she'd met her prince and had lived happily-ever-after. Their relationship hadn't been one of lust but trust and respect, and that was the marriage Poppy wanted. That was truly the ultimate fairy tale. Dal's idea of marriage made her ill, which is why she would never, ever agree to marry him, or to even be a candidate on his "list." She didn't even believe in lists. Or candidates. She believed in love, real love, true love.

And yet his kiss, that kiss, pure magic…

So unbelievably—

No.

No. She wouldn't think about it, not anymore.

Poppy jumped off her bed, unable to remain inside her bedroom a moment longer but not sure where to go, and then glancing out one of her windows, she spotted the enormous lap pool, gleaming with all the pool lights on.

She rifled through her wardrobe until she found the drawer with the swimsuits and grabbed the black bikini with the gold beads on the straps and hips. She topped the suit with a feather-light green gauze tunic and headed downstairs to the long lap pool illuminated for the evening.

Thankfully, there was no one outside, and she could commandeer any one of the dozen lounge chairs.

She picked a chair in the corner and kicked off her leather sandals and peeled off her tunic, dropping them onto the chair before diving into the pool.

She swam under water as far as she could before she had to surface to get air. Turning onto her back

she floated for a moment, feeling some of the tension
melt away.

And then from beneath her lashes, she spotted a
shadowy figure on one of the terraces above, and she
knew from the width of the shoulders who it was.

Poppy turned over onto her stomach and dove back
down, swimming below the surface as if she could
hide from him.

Maybe he didn't see her.

Maybe he'd ignore her.

Somehow she doubted it. There was too much unsettled between them. And that kiss had been so explosive. She'd always wanted to kiss him but that kiss…
that hadn't been what she'd ever imagined.

That kiss had been pure sex, pure sin, and if she
hadn't fled when she did, she would have given herself up to him.

Dal watched Poppy swim in the glowing pool below.

She looked beautiful and sensual floating in the
water, her dark hair glistening in the light of the pool.
He very much wanted to go down and dive in and draw
her toward him, continuing what they started.

She'd feel warm and soft, and slick in the water. He
could imagine cupping her full breasts and then her
rounded derriere.

She was almost naked. He wanted her naked. He
wanted her stripped and exposed so that he could drink
her in.

She was lush and ripe and unbearably sweet. Her
kisses earlier had driven him half-mad. They were ar-
dent and innocent at the same time, and her passion-

ate response had woken a hunger and even now, a half hour later, he still burned.

Everything in him wanted to go down to the pool and take her, and claim her. But he wasn't going to just seduce her. That would be too easy. He wanted her to want him, and want to be with him, but not just for one night. For all nights. Forever.

She needed to marry him. She needed to agree to be his wife.

As his wife, he would spoil her and shower her with gifts and things, endless beautiful things. He'd also give her security and stability. As well as pleasure.

Always pleasure.

But first, the wedding ceremony.

There would be no sex, not until he had his ring on her finger.

CHAPTER SEVEN

POPPY SPENT THE next morning going through the various résumés and applications that had been forwarded, rejecting the ones that would not be a good fit, and then setting aside the possibilities. She even followed up on the references of two different women who'd stood out.

After finishing with the applications, she answered new emails that had come in during the night. There were a few from concerned associates, as well as three very bold inquiries from one member of the press. The reporter was with an American tabloid and asked if Poppy could jump on the phone with her for a quick call, and if that wasn't possible, perhaps Poppy would send a few words…maybe a quote? The online magazine was also quite happy to cite her as an anonymous source, and they did pay, too…all very hush-hush to ensure that the earl would feel no embarrassment.

Poppy deleted the emails from the reporter immediately, determined not to say a word about them to Dal and was just about to close her laptop when an email popped into her inbox from Florrie.

Had such a lovely message from Dal this morning, but having difficulty reaching him on his phone. He said

he has tickets for Royal Box for the Gila Open in Mehkar. Beyond excited. Send me deets, please! And the
poor darling! How is our gorgeous earl holding up?

Poppy read the email twice, unable to believe her eyes.

Dal had been in contact with Florrie now, too. And
he hadn't just checked in with her, he'd dangled VIP
polo tickets to a woman who was completely mad about
ponies.

It was a brilliant move—Dal was nothing if not
shrewd—but also utterly infuriating because just last
night Dal had been seducing her!

Livid, Poppy marched up the flights of stairs, rapped
on his door before entering his room, laptop tucked beneath her arm. "I hope you're dressed," she said curtly,
"because we have work to do."

Dal was lying stretched out on the couch in the liv-
ing room, reading, one arm propped behind his head.
He looked up from the book, a black eyebrow lifting.
"What work would that be?"

"Your work. I get emails about your business affairs all the time. People still think I'm your secretary."

"That's because you are." He sat up, stretching,
which just made the soft knit fabric of his shirt pull
tighter across the hard planes of his chest. "So what is
so urgent?"

She stared at him baffled by his nonchalance. "I
have never seen you lie down in the middle of the day
and read."

"I was focused all morning. Why not take a break
before lunch and get caught up on this book I've been
wanting to read?"

"Indeed?"

"You seem quite tense. Is everything all right?"

"I've just been working for you. That's all."

"Good. Since you're still on the payroll."

She bit her tongue to say something she might regret. And then she had to wait another ten seconds to get her racing pulse to slow. Finally, when she trusted herself to speak and not shout, she said, "I've made good progress on finding my replacement. How is it going finding the replacement for Sophie?"

"Better than I hoped."

"Really?" She decided she'd play dumb. Let him be the one to tell her about his clever invitation to Florrie. "Any exciting developments?"

"Well, I kissed you last night—"

"That's not an exciting development."

The corner of his mouth curled. "It was for me."

"How is it going with the other two on your list?"

"I haven't kissed them, but that's probably due to the lack of proximity and other logistics."

"Would you kiss all three of us if you could?"

"Absolutely."

She hated hearing him say that, she did. Poppy clenched her hands into fists. "Why?"

"Because as you so kindly pointed out, physical attraction is part of marriage—"

"I did not point that out. I said nothing about attraction or sex."

"You did infer that compatibility is important, and part of the 'more' relationships needed."

"Successful relationships."

"Right, and that's what I'm to want for myself because I deserve it. I deserve that elusive 'more.'"

She hated that he kept quoting her, and doing it literally word for word. "'More' is not elusive."

"Isn't it? It's an intangible, something one cannot easily quantify when making an offer, or proposing marriage."

"You should stop talking. You're making me hate you."

"And yet you were the one that told me to communicate. I'm trying to communicate."

"I think you're trying to annoy me."

"Why would I do that?"

"I'm not sure. I haven't figured that part out yet."

"Well, when you do figure it out, let me know. I hate having you upset with me when we only have thirteen days left together."

And just like that she felt her heart mash and fall. She ground her teeth together to keep from making a sound.

"You will be missed," he added kindly. "More than you know."

Poppy smiled to hide how much his reminder hurt. He made her feel crazy, but at least she was able to be crazy and near him. "So you don't need me today? There's nothing you want me to do?"

"Why don't you take the afternoon off? Have some time for yourself. Read or swim or feel free to explore the estate." He was smiling up at her, the smile of a man who acted as if he genuinely cared about her best interests.

He didn't, though. Because if he did, he wouldn't have kissed her like that last night. He wouldn't have held her so firmly, his hands low on her hips, making the inside of her melt and ache, while making the rest of her shiver and tingle. She'd felt his desire, but most of all, she'd become painfully aware of her own. She wanted him...almost desperately. She'd always wanted him, but it had been a cerebral thing, not a body thing, but last night had woken her up and set her body on fire.

Poppy headed for the door, her sandals making a light tapping sound against the marble floor, the tapping echoing the hard, uncomfortable thudding of her heart.

All these years she'd wondered what it would be like to kiss him, and now she knew.

And now she'd never forget.

She paused in the doorway to look back at him. "Oh! Before I forget, Florrie emailed me. She'd love those tickets to the polo match in Gila and is eager for all the *deets*."

And then, flashing him a great, wide, *furious* smile, she walked out.

Dal listened to Poppy's footsteps retreat.

Gone was his tidy, buttoned-up secretary with the tight chignons and conservative skirts and blouses. In her place was this passionate, fierce, fresh-faced beauty who didn't hesitate to give him her opinion. He'd always enjoyed working with Poppy, even when she had her mini meltdowns and crises of confidence, because she was fundamentally one of the best people he'd ever known, but now he enjoyed looking at her. And teasing her. And making her blush.

And shiver and arch in his arms.

She'd been impossibly appealing last night; so appealing that he'd barely been able to sleep, his body heavy and aroused for far too much of the night. Which is why he'd deliberately kept her at arm's length this morning. It had been an endless night and he wasn't ready to be tempted.

But clearly, she didn't like that he'd kept his distance, and she definitely didn't like the email from Florrie.

His lips twisted. Poor Poppy. He'd told Florrie that Poppy would be the one to help her get the tickets because he knew Poppy wouldn't like it.

His smile deepened, remembering her extreme vexation. He wasn't a nice man, but he was good at getting what he wanted, and he wanted Poppy, fierce, passionate, beautiful Poppy, who wasn't afraid to stand up to him, and talk to him and make him feel like a man, not a machine.

Poppy took a bath before dinner feeling incredibly conflicted about the night ahead. At any other time in her life she would have been thrilled at the idea of having a lovely, long evening with him, where it would be just the two of them, but her fantasy Randall was nothing like Sheikh Talal, who did what he wanted and kissed her when he felt like and generally ignored all the rules for polite behavior.

Poppy towel-dried and stepped into the bedroom where Imma had placed a variety of kaftans on the bed for her to choose from.

She wasn't in the mood for the navy or green one, even though both were lovely, and the black looked far too depressing even with all the silver and blue beadwork. She reached for the plum gown with the gold and cream and quickly dressed. She tried drawing her hair into a ponytail but it didn't look right with the formality of the gown. Sighing, Poppy released her hair, combed it hard, hating the thick waves, but left it down.

Imma told her dinner would be on the rooftop and directed her up the three flights of stairs in the central tower. Poppy stepped out of the dim, cool tower into the golden light of dusk, thinking she had never seen a more magical setting for a meal. It was a rooftop dining room, open to the sky. It was heading toward twilight now, but it'd be dark within the hour. The walled patio already gleamed with candlelight, pillars of candles along the waist-high walls, while glittering silver lanterns dotted the side tables.

Stewards stood at attention, one with a tray of cocktails, another with appetizers. A third gentleman held a folded silk pashmina should she become cold later.

It wasn't just luxurious, but wildly romantic, although she'd never tell that to Dal. He was already powerful and overbearing. She didn't need to feed his ego, or his ridiculous marriage plans.

She was not going to marry him. Nor was she on his list. She'd never be on a *list*.

Dal emerged from the opposite tower just a minute after she did. He was wearing elegant black trousers and a fitted black dress shirt open at the collar. He wore no tie and his black hair was combed but he hadn't shaved before dinner, giving him a hint of a shadow on his strong jaw and a wicked glint in his golden eyes.

She hated the shiver that raced down her back, as well as the bubbly, giddy sensation she got when he lifted two glasses from the silver tray, carrying one of the pretty icy-pink cocktails to her. "The Kasbah Jolie signature drink."

"What is it?" she asked warily, taking the frosty glass rimmed in sugar.

"I have no idea. There is a new chef and he seems to be having a great deal of fun naming everything Kasbah this, and Kasbah that."

It seemed that tonight Dal was determined to be charming and she couldn't help smiling. "Cheers to the innovative chefs." And then she clinked her glass to his and sipped the drink, and the icy-cold pink martini-style cocktail was absolutely delicious. She could taste pomegranate juice, grapefruit juice plus vodka and something else. "Compliments to the chef."

"Come this way," he said, taking her elbow and steering her across the enormous roof to a private alcove facing the mountains.

Screened by a hedge of jasmine, he set down his drink and reached into his pocket and drew out a small black velvet box.

Poppy's breath caught in her throat as she spotted what looked like a jeweler's box. This wasn't... it couldn't be...

"I haven't showered you with gifts. I thought it was time," he said. "I hope you like them, and I think you should put them on now."

Like them. Put them on now.

Obviously, it wasn't a ring, then, and she didn't know why she felt a stab of disappointment. She didn't want to marry him. She didn't want to be wooed by him. So why did she care that he was giving her some pretty trinket instead of a diamond ring?

She hated herself for feeling like crying as she cracked open the lid, and catching a sparkle of white fire, she popped the lid open all the way. More glints of light and fire. "Oh, Dal." Nestled in black velvet was a pair of large gold and diamond chandelier earrings, dazzling earrings, the kind that only movie stars and princesses wore. Without even meaning to count, she added up all the diamonds sparkling up at her, with eight large oval diamonds in each earring, with dozens of smaller diamonds covering the gold setting. "I am praying these are not real diamonds," she said.

He looked scandalized. "I have never bought anyone fake stones."

"But these must be a fortune."

"I can afford a fortune." He took one out of the box and loosened the back. "And you deserve a fortune."

"I don't."

"Let's see what they look like on you," he said as though she hadn't spoken. "You're not wearing anything tonight."

"The silver earrings Izba had for me last night wouldn't have looked right with this gown."

"I know. I told her to make sure you couldn't wear the silver earrings tonight."

"You're awfully bossy."

"That shouldn't be news to you," he said, stepping closer so that he put the diamond chandelier on her. His fingertips felt deliciously warm and her ear felt deliciously sensitive. She suppressed a shudder of pleasure as he twisted the back to keep the heavy earring from falling out.

"Now the other ear," he said.

More tingling sensations as he attached the second earring and then gave her head a little shake, hearing the stones click, and feeling the earrings move. "How do they look?"

"You look beautiful."

"I'm afraid this is far too extravagant. I'll wear them tonight, but I can't keep them."

"Don't say things like that. It's not polite."

"You can't give me gifts that cost hundreds of thousands of pounds."

"You're supposed to love them, not argue with me."

"Maybe Florrie and Seraphina like presents like this—"

"Oh, they most definitely do. They wouldn't dream of refusing a token of my affection."

"I'd rather have your real affection."

"You do. You had proof of that last night."

"You're making me very angry," she said.

"Don't be angry. It's a lovely night. Just look at the sunset."

She turned to look out over the valley. The setting sun had painted the red mountains rose, lavender and gold. "It is beyond breathtaking," she said after a moment.

"It is quite spectacular," he agreed. "I wish I hadn't waited so long to return. It's good to be back."

She glanced up at him. "Did you think it wouldn't?"

In the elegant black evening shirt, his skin looked more olive and his eyes appeared an even lighter gold. It was funny how she'd always thought of him as so very English, and yet here in Mehkar, he exuded heat and mystery, as well as an overwhelming sensuality.

"I was worried," he admitted after a moment. "I was worried about what it'd be like here without Andrew and my mother. I'd never been here without them, but you've made it easy for me."

"Are you going to see your grandfather while we're here?"

"I should, but haven't made any plans to do so yet."

"Tell me about your relationship with him."

"There's not much to understand. I live in England. He lives in Mehkar."

"And yet you're here in Mehkar, and we were in Gila, albeit briefly."

"It's complicated," he said brusquely.

"That's your code for you don't want to discuss it."

"It really is complicated. I don't even know how to talk about it. One day this place was my home. It was my favorite place in the world. And then suddenly it wasn't part of my life anymore, and the people here were cut off, too. It was bad enough losing my mum and brother, but to lose your grandparents and cousins and aunts and uncles? It hurt more than I can say. It's still not easy to talk about."

"Who cut them off? Your father or your grandfather?"

He shoved a hand through his black hair, rifling it. "Does it matter?"

She looked down into the shimmering pink of her cocktail, the color so very similar to the walls of the Kasbah. "I guess I have this crazy idea that if I understand your past, then maybe I'll understand you."

He gave her a look she couldn't decipher. "I've spent all these years burying the memories. I don't know that it's wise to dig them all up."

"Buried memories mean buried emotions—"

"My favorite kind," he said darkly.

"Don't you want to feel anything?"

"No. But apparently, you do." He finished his drink and set the glass down on the wall next to his hip. "It was June eleventh. We'd just finished the school term and were out on holiday. Mum came to pick us up, as she always did. We were on our way to the airport to come here when the accident happened." He paused before saying slowly, clearly. "The accident that killed my mother and Andrew."

It took her a moment to piece it together. "You were on your way here? To Jolie?"

"We always flew here straightaway on our last day of school. It was our tradition. We couldn't wait to come. At least I couldn't wait. Andrew had wanted to stay home that summer with Father but Mother insisted. Grandfather wanted to see Andrew." He frowned, brows flattening. "Andrew was the oldest of my grandfather's grandchildren, important to both sides of the family."

He looked up right into her eyes, expression still intense. "Until that day, I'd had a very different childhood from Andrew. He was the heir. I was just a boy…a free-spirited, rather sensitive, second son."

She didn't know what to say, so she didn't try to speak.

Dal added after a moment, "It wasn't ever the same after that. Not in Winchester. Not here."

"It wouldn't be, would it?" she said sympathetically before adding, "So you chose not to come back?"

"It was my father's decision to cut contact with my mother's family. After the funerals, I didn't see or hear from anyone from Mehkar for ten years."

"Why?"

"My father blamed my mother for the accident, and so by extension, he blamed her family."

"Was she at fault?"

"No. The other driver was distracted. They said he

was on the phone, ran a red light and smashed into our car head-on."

"Mother died immediately. Andrew died at the hospital. And I survived with just cuts and bruises."

"Your poor grandfather," she sighed. "It must have been devastating to lose his daughter and his eldest grandson on the very day they were to return home."

"I'm sure it wasn't easy for him. My grandmother, his wife, had died just months before in an accident. He'd been eager to have my mother return for the summer."

"So your grandfather has never reached out to you since your mother's funeral. If you were eleven that has been nearly twenty-four years!"

"No. He reached out. I was rude. I rebuffed him, and even though I was at fault, I have chosen not to apologize or make amends."

"Why?"

"I don't know."

"I don't believe that. I think you do know. And I'd like to know."

"So you can have additional proof of what a cool, unfeeling ass I am?"

She gave him a reproving look. "I already know who you are, and what you are, which is why I want to know why you—someone I know does have feelings, only you keep them very deeply buried—would rebuff someone you apparently once loved very much?"

His shoulders shifted impatiently. "Because I did love him. And I didn't understand why he left me there, in England. I hated England. I hated my father—" He broke off, jaw grinding, shadows darkening his eyes. "It doesn't matter, and I shouldn't admit that I hated my father. My father had problems. He couldn't help himself."

"But you can help yourself. Reach out to your grandfather. See him. Apologize. Make amends."

"I can't."

"You *can*. Don't be stupid and proud. Tell him you're sorry, because one day he won't be here and then it'll be too late."

Dal didn't say anything for the longest time. He finished his drink and she finished hers and they watched the shadows swaddle the mountains, the rose and gold light fading to lavender and gray.

After a long silence Dal glanced at her, lips curving. "You're the only person that ever tries to tell me what to do."

"You could be a really, truly lovely man if you tried."

"That sounds terribly dull."

"I like dull men. I'm looking for a dull man, someone who will cuddle with me on the sofa while we watch our favorite program on the telly."

"You would hate that after a while."

"Not if it was a good program."

"You almost make watching television sound fun."

Fun. In all her years of working for him, she'd never once heard him the use the word *fun.* Discipline, duty, responsibility, yes. But fun? Never. "You have changed," she said. "You're already very different from just a few days ago."

"It seems I had to. Randall Grant was an arse."

"Is Dal better?"

"He's trying."

She glanced at him from beneath her lashes and felt a little shiver as he looked right back at her, his golden gaze locking with hers and holding. He didn't look away, not even when one of the stewards invited them to the dinner table.

"Why didn't you try before?" she asked softly. "Why didn't you try for Sophie?"

"I don't know. Maybe because she didn't bring out the best in me. Not like you."

"I bring out the best in you?"

His dense black lashes dropped, his lovely mouth curving. "Perhaps I should say you bring out the *better*."

Her chest squeezed, her insides wobbly. He made her feel so much and it wasn't fair. When he dropped his guard and had a real conversation she felt close to him. Connected. *Too connected.* How was she to leave him when he felt like hers?

One of the stewards approached them and spoke quietly in Arabic to Dal. Dal answered and then turned to Poppy. "I have a phone call I must take. It won't take long, just a couple minutes. Please have another drink and I'll meet you at the table."

True to his word, he was gone less than ten minutes, and when he returned she was waiting at the beautiful table with the rose-pink tablecloth and the gleaming white candles.

"I tried to make it quick," he said, sitting down at the table with her.

"Is everything okay?"

"It was Florrie."

Poppy's chest squeezed tight. "Oh?"

"She's heading to Gila for the polo tournament and she had some questions about the tournament and packing and appropriate dress for the royal box."

"I didn't realize you were a fashion consultant."

He leaned back in his chair, his lips quirking. "You're jealous."

"I'm not."

"No, you shouldn't be. I've asked you to marry me—"

"You've never asked. You told me we were to marry. That's not a proper proposal."

"So is that all that's keeping you from saying yes? Are you wanting romance? Flowers? Candlelight?"

She became very aware of the romantic dinner under the stars, and the fragrant roses on the table, along with the candles glimmering everywhere.

"You threw your list together," she said. "There was very little thought put into it, and I wish you would have considered more possibilities. Women who are not Sophie's friends. Women who might actually want to stay at home with you and have dinner with you, or maybe grab a book and read in the evening near you—"

"I don't need a nanny, Poppy."

"No, you just need a woman with hips and a womb."

When he didn't contradict her, she felt her temper spike. "You are so infuriating! You know you haven't tried hard to find a great wife. You're simply settling—"

"Not settling at all. You're on the list."

"At the number three position, which makes me think that the names on your list are there by default. I'd hazard to guess that all three names made it because that's all you could remember in a pinch."

He grinned at her, a sexy, powerful, masculine smile. "Your name was not added because I was in a pinch. *You* were added because we suit each other—"

"So annoying," she muttered under her breath.

"Why can't you accept a compliment?"

"Because I know you. You don't compliment people, and you most certainly don't compliment *me*."

"Let me put it another way. I can barely tolerate most people but I haven't just tolerated your company for the past four years. I've enjoyed it."

"And you wonder why I have absolutely no desire to marry you!"

"It wouldn't hurt for you to be a little more logical and a lot less fanciful."

"How about we focus on the two women still on your list? You can't court both Florrie and Seraphina at the same time. It's not practical when you're down to fourteen days, and so I recommend at this point in time you focus on one. With Florrie en route to Gila, just settle on her and be done with it. I am sure once she learns that you're not just the Earl of Langston but Prince Talal she'll jump through the hoops and marry you right away."

"I had no idea Florrie was your clear favorite."

"She's not my favorite. In fact, of the two, she's my least favorite."

"Is she? Why?"

"She's—" *The least monogamous woman I know.* But Poppy bit back the words, uncomfortable with the truth. "She just doesn't seem quite ready to settle down."

"I don't know. Maybe she hasn't yet met the right person."

"Maybe," Poppy answered sourly.

"What else do you know about them? Who would I enjoy more? No. Scratch that. Which one would be a more natural mother?"

Poppy shuddered. "Neither. They are both too self-absorbed."

"You're sounding very catty right now, Poppy. It's not attractive. I thought these were your friends."

"Sophie's friends."

"Is there nothing positive you can say about either?"

Poppy ground her teeth together and lifted her chin. "Seraphina loves fashion and clothes. She spends twenty thousand or more each season on new clothes."

"You're supposed to be giving me positives."

"That is a positive. She's always beautifully dressed. Oh. And she keeps herself very slender. Very, very slender."

"Is that your way of saying she has an eating disorder?"

"No. It's my way of saying she just doesn't eat. She has a liquid diet. Mostly green drinks and cleansers. Things like that."

"I'm sure she'd indulge in cheese plates and chocolate now and then."

Poppy frowned, trying to remember when she'd ever seen Seraphina actually eat anything. She nearly always had a bottle in her hand, or purse, filled with one of those drinks that smelled of lemon and parsley, cucumber and ginger. "I've never actually seen her eat anything sweet. Or anything with carbs. Or any kind of meat."

"So she won't share a steak and kidney pie with me?"

"Oh, no. Never. The crust alone would make her faint."

"What about Florrie? Would she eat a steak and kidney pie?"

"Probably."

"That's good news."

"Yes." But Poppy couldn't feign enthusiasm. Florrie would not be a good wife for Dal. She wasn't even a good girlfriend. She didn't understand the meaning of faithful, juggling her polo player lovers with disconcerting ease.

"Now, come on, Poppy. What's wrong with Florrie? If I didn't know you better, I'd think you were jealous and wanted to be my countess."

He was right, of course. She was jealous, but she'd never let him know that. "Fortunately, you do know me better and know I've absolutely zero desire to be your countess."

"Why?"

"I hate that you dangle money and possessions and make it sound as if those material things are the basis for a good marriage, when we both know that nothing is more important than affection, kindness and respect."

"If I wasn't the Earl of Langston, but a vicar in a Cotswold parish, would you consider my proposal?"

Her cheeks burned with embarrassment but she held his gaze. "If you were a vicar in the Cotswold, would you love me?"

"I don't know how to answer because I don't believe in love. It's a fantasy concocted in the twentieth century by advertising giants to sell more things to more people."

"That is such rubbish."

"But I do believe passion and desire are real."

"And I believe that passion without love is just sex. And I wouldn't ever marry a man just to have sex. I could have sex *now* if that's what I wanted."

"Sex with whom?"

She lifted her chin, absolutely brazen. "You."

Her words stole his breath. And all rational thought. Her eyes shone with light while her cheeks glowed with color and her expression was nothing short of defiant.

Who was this woman? When had she become so confident and provocative?

It didn't help that the lush outline of Poppy's breast was playing havoc with his control.

He'd managed his physical side for five and a half years, clamping down tightly on all needs or wants, shutting himself down so that he could be the elegant, chivalrous man Sophie desired.

But with Sophie gone, and Poppy here, he felt anything but elegant and chivalrous.

What he felt was ravenous, his carnal side awake and hungry. After years of not feeling or wanting or needing, he needed now. He needed her. And his body ached morning, noon and night with desire.

Just watching her bite her full lower lip now made him want to kiss that tender lip, and then lick the seam of her lips so that she'd open for him and let him have his way with her.

His tongue in her mouth.

His tongue on her breasts.

His tongue between her legs, lathing her clit.

Dal hardened all over again, his skin so tight he felt like he'd explode.

"You have no idea what I want to do to you," he said huskily, picturing stripping her naked so that her full breasts were bared, her nipples peaked. He'd work her nipples, pinching, teasing, sucking, until she was wet for him and arching, hips lifting, begging.

He wanted to be between her thighs.

He wanted to clasp her hips and hold her still while he devoured her.

He wanted to feel her shattering and hear her cry and know that she was his, and only his.

"Not interested," she said. "I don't want to sleep with you, or marry you. You're not my type—"

"You don't have a type, Poppy. You haven't dated once in all the years you've worked for me."

"Not true. I had a boyfriend three years ago—"

"A boyfriend?"

"Yes. A boyfriend. He was lovely, too, until well, he wasn't so lovely anymore."

"And just how long was he your boyfriend?"

"I don't remember."

"That means he wasn't around long enough to truly signify."

"That's not what it means. It just means I decided to move forward and put the past behind me."

"I have a feeling he was your boyfriend for all of three weeks."

"It's not really any of your business whether he was my boyfriend for three minutes or three years. What matters is that I don't want to be your girlfriend, or your wife, or anything at all because your values are not my values. You don't want what I want in life. We'd be a disaster together."

"Even though you like how I can make you feel?"

Color stormed her cheeks and her eyes snapped fire. "You must be confusing me with someone else on your list because I care about you, and yes, I enjoyed kissing you last night, but I'm not going to give up my free-dom and future just because I felt a twinge of lust!"

CHAPTER EIGHT

BACK IN HER ROOM, Poppy allowed Imma to help her ease the stunning plum kaftan off her head. While Imma hung the gorgeous gown back up, Poppy removed her dangling gold and diamond earrings, tucking them into a drawer next to her bed before taking off her makeup.

But even a half hour after changing into her pajamas, she felt hot and riled up. Dal was beyond annoying. He was the worst. The absolute worst.

Poppy stripped off her nightgown and put on her swimsuit and cover-up, and headed for the pool.

She swam a lap under water, and then another lap under water before surfacing to float on her back.

The warm water soothed her, relaxing her tense muscles, while the gentle lap of water against her skin made her feel buoyant and free.

She heard a scraping sound and opened her eyes to discover Dal sitting down on the foot of her lounge chair.

He was still dressed for dinner, which reassured her somewhat because that meant he wasn't planning on swimming. Maybe if she closed her eyes and ignored him, he'd leave soon.

She flipped over onto her stomach and did a slow, easy breaststroke toward the opposite end of the pool. She pretended she was alone, without a care in the world, even though she could feel his eyes, his gaze, following her every kick and stroke.

At the far end she reached for the wall and turned around, facing him.

He looked at her, his handsome face expressionless.

She almost wished for one of his small, mocking smiles. The smiles and ironic laughter were easier than this tension between them now.

"What do you want?" she called, even as she stretched her arms out along the tiled pool edge, and leaned back so her legs could float up.

"You."

"But I don't want you."

"Liar."

The low, husky pitch of his voice sent shivers racing through her, making her tummy clench and her knees press tight.

She couldn't engage, couldn't encourage him; it would be disastrous to provoke him at this late hour.

Poppy forced herself to relax. She closed her eyes, let herself float where she was, and as she breathed in and out, she pictured him getting up and walking away. In fact, she willed him to leave, pouring all her concentration into making him disappear, but when she opened her eyes, he was still there.

"I can prove it to you," he said.

"We're not children. There's no need to prove anything to anyone."

"You can't hide forever from the truth."

"But I can get some laps in, can't I?"

"I'll wait."

"I have a lot of laps."

"I'll count them for you."

She shot him a frosty look, not comfortable with this game.

She dove under water and swam half the length of the pool before needing to surface for a breath. When she glanced over her shoulder toward the lounge chair where she'd left her things, she realized he was gone. For a split second she felt relief, and then she noticed the pile of clothes set next to her tunic on the lounge chair.

He'd undressed.

Poppy spun in the pool, discovering him behind her. "What are you doing?" she demanded breathlessly.

"Joining you for a swim."

"Are you...naked?" she asked, afraid to look down.

"Have you never gone skinny-dipping?"

"No." Her voice came out strangled. "So you are naked."

"Would you feel better if I told you I was wearing briefs?"

"Yes."

"Then I'm wearing briefs," he answered, reaching for her and drawing her toward him with the assurance of a man who knew exactly what he was doing. He drew her through the water until her breasts brushed his chest.

His body was so large and warm, and it felt unbelievably good to be pressed to him, skin to skin. Her breath caught when his large hands circled her waist, drawing her hips even closer to his.

He wasn't naked. But he was hard...very thick and

very erect. Her eyes widened as he rubbed her across him, the tip of his shaft finding the apex of her thighs and all the sensitive nerves there.

Her lips parted. She made a soft hiss of sound.

He lifted an eyebrow. "Did you say something?"

"This isn't a good idea," she choked, even as he did it again, and the thick blunt tip against her core made her want to swoon.

Maybe he wasn't wearing briefs after all…

"I don't think this is a good idea," she said hoarsely, even as her pulse raced and her skin felt exquisitely sensitive.

"We're just playing," he said.

She stared at him, mesmerized, at the gleam of water on his shadowed jaw, and the way the pool light reflected onto the hard features of his face. "But this kind of play is dangerous."

"You're safe with me."

"I don't think that's true at all." In fact, she knew it wasn't true, and yet it was hard to move away from him when everything in her wanted this with every fiber of her being.

But that didn't make it right, a tiny part of her brain shrieked. Sugar is delicious, but too much will make you sick.

And he most definitely wasn't sugar.

He was spice, wicked, sexy spice and beyond addictive.

"You want danger," he murmured, his lips brushing her ear, and then finding the hollow below.

Pleasure shrieked through her and she gasped, lips pressing to the warm wall of his chest.

"But you want danger that won't destroy you," he

added, his teeth catching at her earlobe and giving it a tug. "And you know I would never destroy you. I'd just teach you all the things you've always wanted to know."

"Like what?"

"This," he answered, his head dropping so that his mouth covered hers in a light, teasing kiss. Last night's kiss had been fierce and hot, but this kiss was tender and light and unbearably erotic.

His lips brushed hers, and then again, sending ripples of pleasure from her lips into her breasts and belly and beyond.

The fleeting caress seemed to wake nerve endings she didn't even know she had and she lifted her mouth to his, wanting more.

She felt his smile as he kissed her, his lips just barely parting hers, and the tip of his tongue lightly touching the inside of her lower lip.

Oh, that felt so good. Goose bumps covered her arm and made the fine damp hair at her nape rise. Her breasts swelled, aching, too.

"One more of those," she pleaded.

The soft, warm kiss flooded her with heat, and then as his tongue did a slow, lazy exploration of her mouth she pressed herself closer, thinking it was just a kiss and yet so much more.

She wanted so much more.

And when his hand moved to her breast, playing with the taut nipple through her wet suit, she nearly groaned at the pleasure. His hand felt so good on her, and the way he touched her sensitive nipple made her tummy tighten and her lower back prickle as she felt close to popping out of her skin.

"And you say desire isn't important," Dal said, lifting his head to look into her eyes.

She blushed and tried not to squirm as he tugged and kneaded her nipple, each small pull creating more tension inside her and adding to the heat between her thighs. "Desire is important," she whispered breathlessly as he pinched and played with her, the sensation so new and erotic that she couldn't focus properly.

"So you agree."

"I agree it's part of love."

"You can desire someone you do not love."

"Well, I couldn't," she answered, gasping as he pushed the scrap of fabric covering her breast away, exposing her nipple.

She saw his eyes darken in appreciation, his hard jaw jutting just before he bent his head and took the tender pebbled peak in his mouth.

His mouth felt surprisingly cool against her warm skin, and then as he suckled her she grew hot and wet in a way that had nothing to do with the pool or the warm, cloudless night. She clung more tightly to him, her fingers biting into his shoulders as her body came to life, shivering and shuddering from the intense sensation streaking through her.

She strained to be closer, seeking more contact and more friction. As he drew on her nipple, she pressed her hips to him, wanting the rough rasp of his chest hair and the thick press of his erection.

He wrapped her legs around his waist, securing her ankles behind his back. "Don't move," he commanded.

"You're not in charge—" she began to protest but then broke off as his fingers slipped inside her bikini bottoms, finding the cleft where she was so wet and hot.

She shuddered as he stroked her there, finding her tender nub and then down and circling back again. He then drew his fingers away, and he looked down at her, a black brow lifting.

Her hips rocked helplessly. She felt beyond bereft, her core clenching, her body straining for touch, for relief.

"Are you in charge, then?" he asked quietly, silkily, combing her dark, wet hair back from her face.

Her cheeks burned. She burned. She felt as if he'd set her on fire and was now watching her incinerate.

"Maybe I spoke too soon," she said faintly.

"Louder?"

"You are in charge. There. Happy?"

"Not yet. But I will be, soon."

And then he slipped his hand back beneath the elastic of her bikini panty, stroking between her thighs, learning the shape of her. It was all very nice but she wanted him to do what he'd done before. Touch her there, at that place where all the nerve endings seemed to be.

She opened her thighs wider, pressing her hips at him, unable to ask for what she wanted, but he didn't seem in a hurry to caress the nub. Instead, he traced the outer lips and then inner lips before slipping the tip of his finger inside her. She hissed a breath, lips parting as he withdrew and then did it again, just touching her with the tip, making her shudder, making her want to press his finger deeper.

"It will sting when I possess you on our wedding night," he said, kissing the side of her neck, finding more sensitive spots she didn't know existed. "But it will only hurt that first night."

"We're not marrying," she breathed, twitching as he found her nub and gave it a caress.

"You should give up now," he said, stroking the nub again, making her tighten and dance against him. "You won't win."

"You can't buy me, and you can't seduce me," she choked.

"Maybe I can't buy you, but I can seduce you. I am seducing you." And then as he caressed her clit, he slipped the fingertip back inside her, making her whimper.

He deftly stroked both, and she didn't know which pleasure to focus on. Both sensations felt so good, the bright, sharp pleasure at the top of her thighs, or the sensitive shivers from teasing her below.

She felt her body try to tighten around his finger, the sensations so new and exciting but also overwhelming.

He kissed her then, and she wrapped her arms more tightly around his neck, kissing him back. He sucked her tongue into his mouth, drawing on her tongue in a tight, hot, erotic rhythm that had her hips rotating. She felt like she was on fire, sensation flooding her. It was hard to focus on any one pleasure when it all felt so good together—her tongue in his mouth, his hand between her thighs, stroking her. She felt the pressure build and tighten, everything in her tensing, and then he slipped a finger inside her even as his thumb played across her nub and suddenly she couldn't control the pleasure, couldn't keep it together, and she cried out against his mouth, shattering in her first climax ever.

For long moments after, she was breathless and

dazed. She felt boneless and weak and she rested her head against his chest as he rearranged her in his arms, letting her legs settle and her body relax. Another few moments later, she felt sufficiently recovered to push away, needing distance now, uncomfortable with what had just happened.

"Do you have a preference for the kind of ring you'd like?" he asked.

Poppy blinked, her brain still fuzzy and disconnected from the pleasure. "Ring?"

"I'll give you the ring tomorrow, and we'll marry a week from today. That gives us a full week before my birthday. I don't want to leave it to the last minute this time."

"That is surely the least romantic proposal I have ever heard of in my life."

"I gave you romance at dinner. I just proved we have chemistry. And there is a great deal of it between us. Now we just need to finalize the details so we can move forward with our lives—"

"You're mad," she interrupted, floating farther away.

"Possibly. It runs in the family."

"Don't say that. It's not funny." Poppy had first learned of Randall's father's illness from the housekeeper at Langston House years ago. The housekeeper had wanted Poppy to understand why control was so important to the Sixth Earl of Langston. It seemed that the Fifth Earl had none.

"I'm entirely serious. My father was quite ill."

"I know."

"Sophie told you?"

"I don't think Sophie knows."

"But you do?"

"Mrs. Holmes told me."

"Why would she do that?"

"It was the day after your father's funeral. You'd told me to return to London and she asked me not to go."

"Why? Was she afraid I'd hurt myself?"

Poppy flinched. "No. She just didn't want you alone. She thought you needed a friend with you."

"And you were my friend?"

She lifted her chin, unwilling to let him see he'd hurt her. "I was the only one there. You'd managed to scare everyone else off."

"You make me sound like a monster."

She heard the bruised note in his voice. She glanced away, over the sparkling surface of the water, trying to think of something to say.

"Sophie used to call me the Ice Monster." His voice had grown even deeper. "You used to laugh."

"It was that or cry," she flashed, glancing down at her hands skimming back and forth just below the surface of the water. "But I'm no Belle, and you're no Beast and I can't save you—"

"Not asking you to save me. I'm asking you to marry me."

"In your case, it's one and the same, isn't it? You don't want me. You don't even want to marry. You're just trying to protect your title and lands."

When he didn't answer, she persisted. "Is it really so terrible to lose the earldom and estates?"

"Yes."

"Why? You don't need the money. And you don't seem to care at all for the title. If you have all this here in Mehkar, why do you need Langston House and the rest? Most of your investments aren't tied to the property, and the title is just a title."

Good for Poppy for asking the question. But then, he would have been surprised if she'd hadn't eventually asked it.

He certainly would have asked it if he were her, because she was right. The income wasn't significant, and Dal wasn't attached to the title, but the house was his home and then there was the real issue, the issue of duty. The issue of commitment and honor. Responsibility.

Duty and responsibility had been drummed into him every single day following his mother and brother's funeral.

His brother Andrew had understood duty. His brother, Viscount Andrew Ulrich Mansur Grant, was to have been the Sixth Earl of Langston, and Andrew loved everything about being the firstborn. He understood the responsibility but he didn't find it crushing. He knew he'd one day marry someone who benefited the estate, rather than someone he fancied. He would have been an excellent earl, too.

Dal had not been a good replacement for his brother. He was hapless—the Fifth Earl's description—and overly intellectual, so his father had been forced to shape Dal into a proper heir, even if it broke both of them.

And it had nearly broken both of them.

"From the time I was eleven, I understood my sole life mission was to marry and have children. Not just an heir and a spare, but numerous spares in the event something awful happened." He lifted his head, his gaze finding Poppy's. "Because awful things did happen. Cars crashed and mothers died and older brothers die in hospitals during surgery."

"Heirs and spares," he added mockingly, bitingly, "were not children to be loved, but insurance policies. Annoying but essential."

Wives were not to be cherished, either. They were brood mares, and income. The Grants of Langston had filled their coffers for the past hundred and fifty years by marrying foreign heiresses: Greek, American, German and in the case of Randall's mother, Arab. The wife didn't have to be beautiful, or even accomplished. According to the Fifth Earl of Langston, Randall's wife needed to be healthy—to bear those heirs—and wealthy. Her dowry was the most important thing she brought to the marriage.

Randall had been shocked and disgusted as a boy, but the years of lectures and discipline had numbed him to all but duty. Duty was the only thing that mattered, because once he fulfilled his duty, he would be free, no longer haunted by the fact that it was Andrew who should have been the Sixth Earl, not he.

"Who I am in Mehkar has no bearing on who I am in England, nor does it change my duty. My duty is to marry and continue the Grant family. It's my sole responsibility. I've known since my mother and brother's funeral that I have no other reason for being alive."

"That is probably the vilest thing I have ever heard you say."

He shrugged. "I will fulfill the promise made to my father, not to save the land or pocket the income, but because I am determined to get this monkey off my back."

"It's not a monkey, it's a curse!"

"I won't let it be a curse in the future. I'm a different man than my father and I'll make different choices." He hesitated. "You have no idea how different I want the future to be, and with you, it will be a new future. With you, I can move on."

"I hear about what you need, but what about what I need? Or do women not matter in your world? Are we just things…property and possessions?"

"You want security in life, and I'm offering it to you."

"You're not offering security. You're taking my freedom and the opportunities before me."

"I can take you places, show you the world."

"I don't want the world. I want a comfortable little house and a garden where I can plant my flowers."

"And in that house there will be a couch, and a telly and a husband that will kiss and cuddle you."

"Yes."

"You have not spent the past four years working for me to sit with some fat, balding bloke who only wants to watch football—"

"He's not going to be fat, or balding, and he's most definitely not going to be obsessed with football." Her chin jerked up. "He will be obsessed with me."

"Right."

"I'm serious."

"It will never happen."

"Why not?"

"Because you're going to marry me, and be my wife, and we're going to have the life you wanted…the life we wanted…the life where you insisted we have more!"

"Marrying you would not be more. Marrying you would be less."

"Coward!"

"Your idea of marriage makes my skin crawl."

"Liar."

"Listen to me. Listen, Randall Michael Talal Grant, Earl of Langston, Sheikh of Mehkar, I have no desire to be your countess, or your princess. I fancied you, yes. I had a crush on you, yes. But I never once wanted to trade places with Sophie because I knew then what I still know now. You will never love anyone but yourself. You can't. You don't know how."

CHAPTER NINE

SHE HEARD THE helicopter early, just after dawn. Poppy left her bed to stumble to the window arriving just in time to see the black helicopter with the gold emblem rise from the gardens, lifting straight up.

She saw the pilot, and then she spotted Dal in the backseat.

She felt a shaft of pain. Where was he going? And why was he leaving her here?

She struggled to breathe as the helicopter flew away, her chest unnaturally tight.

It had been an awful night. She hadn't been able to sleep, not after the terrible fight with Dal in the pool.

She'd said hurtful things to him, and she'd regretted them immediately. She'd spent much of the night lying awake, wanting to go to him and apologize, but pride and self-preservation kept her in her bed.

If she went to him, she'd apologize and then possibly kiss him, and if she kissed him, then she'd want him to touch her, and hold her and then it would be all over.

He'd win. And she couldn't let him win. This wasn't a business deal. This wasn't a financial transaction. This was about her life and her future. It was about all the values she held dear: love, and hope and faith.

Love, hope, faith and family.

He'd give her the children but he couldn't give her the other things she craved.

And so she'd forced herself to stay in her bed, aware that Dal was upset, but it wasn't her problem. She cared about him—oh, so very much—but she couldn't allow him to just ride roughshod all over her.

But oh, last night…

She tipped her head to the glass and closed her eyes. His proposal had been so incredibly uncomfortable. And her furious refusal, that was even more uncomfortable.

So where had he gone today? What was he thinking? What was he doing?

Poppy dressed and went to her living room and rang for coffee. It was Izba who came to the door, not Imma or Hayek.

"Where did Talal go?" Poppy asked her.

"Gila."

"Gila," Poppy repeated numbly. "Did he say how long he'd be gone?"

The old woman's face creased. "Three days. Maybe four. He said there is a big tournament in the city. Polo, I think he said." She tipped her head, expression curious. "You don't like polo, Miss Poppy?"

Poppy felt a lump fill her throat. "No," she answered huskily. "Not as much as some women I know."

So he'd gone to Gila. Gone to Gila to see Florrie.

Poppy felt ill, so ill that she stripped off her clothes and climbed back into bed.

She heard the helicopter late on the third night after he'd gone. Poppy glanced at the small clock next to her bed. Nearly midnight.

Relief filled her. Relief followed by pain.

He'd left her three days ago and he hadn't said good-bye. He hadn't emailed her, either, even though she'd checked her inbox obsessively.

But now he was back home.

And then she realized what she'd thought. Home.

She turned on her side, pulling the cover up over her shoulder as if she could tuck herself in. But even beneath the covers she was cold. And scared. Had he proposed to Florrie? Or God help her, had he married Florrie while he was there?

She tried to make herself fall back asleep but she couldn't. She lay in bed, heart pounding, stomach knotting, so anxious. So heartsick.

A half hour passed, and then another. It was close to one in the morning now but she was wide awake and close to tears.

Unable to endure another moment of misery, she left her bed and pulled on a pale green cotton robe and headed for Dal's suite one floor above hers.

She knocked on the door. There was no answer. She gently turned the handle and it opened. She entered the living room, crossing soundlessly the long narrow living room to his bedroom. The door there was open and she stepped inside his bedroom, her gaze going to his bed. It was empty, the bed made. A lamp was burning on a corner table and the sliding glass door was open.

"Dal?" she whispered.

She saw a shadow move on the balcony and then he appeared in the doorway.

"What's wrong?" he asked.

"I couldn't sleep. I was worried about you."

"As you can see I'm fine."

She reached for the sash on her robe, giving it an anxious tug. "How was Gila?"

"Good."

"What did you do there?"

"I saw a lot of family. I think I forgot just how big the family is."

"Were you able to spend time with your grandfather?"

"Yes."

"Did you attend the polo match?"

"I went for a little while."

He just went for part of the match? What else did he do, then? And did he see Florrie? Did he take her out on a date? Did he kiss—?

Poppy stopped herself there, not wanting to imagine all the possibilities. Not even wanting to know if there had been a date. Too much could happen, and the details would just make her feel half-mad.

"You were gone for three days," she said, hearing the hurt and accusation in her voice but it was too late to take the words back.

He shrugged. "I had things to take care of. Arrangements to make."

For his wedding.

He hadn't said the words, but she was sure of it. Pain exploded inside her chest, and she balled her hands, her nails digging into her fists. "Is there anything I can help with?"

"No, you're doing what I needed you to do. You've given me five strong résumés. Someone from HR in the London office will call the five, interview and then rank them for me, and then hire the one they think is the strongest."

As her eyes adjusted to the night, she could see he was leaning on the frame of the glass door, his shoulder at an angle, muscular arms crossed over his bare chest. He was wearing dark, loose pajama bottoms. He had such a big, hard, gorgeous body and his mind was brilliant—sharp, swift, incisive. She'd loved working with him, and learning from him and hearing his ideas. He was bold and brave, conscientious and fair. His new secretary was going to be very lucky to have him as a boss. "Sounds as if my job is nearly done."

"Indeed. We will probably have someone hired by the end of this week."

She swallowed around the lump in her throat. "It's all coming to an end so fast now."

"It seems everything is working out."

"Does that include your search for a new bride?"

"Yes."

"You must be relieved."

"I'll be relieved when the wedding is over."

"Do you have a date set?"

"I don't want to leave it to the last moment."

"You have nine days until your birthday."

"Yes, so probably three or four days from now." His big shoulders shifted. "Something like that."

So soon.

"That's wonderful," she said even as she found herself wishing she hadn't come here, to his room. She should have waited until morning to ask about his trip. She could have waited to hear this news.

She hated his news. It broke her heart. "Was it good to speak to your grandfather?"

"Yes. Just seeing him again has made the trip here worthwhile."

"I'm glad." She swallowed again, fighting the prickle and sting of tears in the backs of her eyes. "Did you tell your grandfather about your plans to marry?"

"Yes."

"What did he say?"

"He said that he respected me for fulfilling the promise I made my father, and hoped that my future wife will bring honor to the family and the people of Mehkar."

"Have you introduced her to him yet?"

"No, and I won't. Not before the ceremony. This is my choice, not his, and I'm not looking for his approval."

She was silent a moment, trying to imagine Dal with his grandfather, the king. "What is he like? Your grandfather?"

"Perceptive. Powerful. Quiet. Dignified."

"Easy to talk to?"

He laughed softly. "He wasn't at first, but by the time I left, it was better. He has aged. He has worries." He straightened and entered the room. "I suppose we all do."

She watched him cross the floor and take a seat on the side of his bed. "What are you worrying about?"

"My worries are mostly behind me. I've done what I needed to do. Now I can breathe easier." He looked at her. "I'm just sorry you lost sleep over me. That must have been truly aggravating."

"Don't be angry with me."

"I'm not. I'm not angry with you, or anyone. I think for the first time in years, I'm finally at peace."

She wanted to ask him why. She wanted to know if Florrie was wearing his engagement ring. She wanted to know so many things but knew she didn't have the right to ask anymore. She'd essentially found her replacement. She wouldn't be working for him soon. He'd be married to Florrie—

"I hated you leaving the way you did," she whispered. "And then you didn't even email me once."

"I was busy."

"You were punishing me."

"If there is to be no future together, we need to create distance. I left to give us distance, and allow us both to take a step back."

"Is that why you're at peace?"

"I'm at peace because I know, no matter what happens in the next week, I have the answers I need." He reached up to drag a hand through his thick hair, ruffling it. "In Gila, my grandfather and I talked quite a lot about my father. My grandfather had offered to bring my mother home from England more than once, wanting to rescue her from her difficult marriage. She refused. She believed my father needed her, and that it wouldn't be fair to take the children away from him, and so she stayed."

"Your poor mother."

"That is what I always thought, but my grandfather said my mother loved him. Apparently, she was the only one who could manage him." He smiled grimly. "Rather like you with me."

"You're not a monster."

"He didn't want to be, either."

"Don't compare yourself to him! You're not your father. He had struggles you don't have. His mood swings, and mania, that was his illness. It's not yours."

"Emotions make me uncomfortable."

"Because of him."

"His emotions were out of control, so I trained myself never to lose control."

All of a sudden she understood. "You're not him, Dal. You're not ever going to be him. And you didn't inherit the illness, either."

"But my children could."

She felt another sharp stab of pain. My God. She'd never thought of that, or imagined that he'd harbor secret fears that his children could. "Or not," she said quietly, evenly, finally seeing what she'd never seen before.

"I spent my twenties waiting for the disease to strike. I kept waiting for signs or symptoms…highs, lows, anger, despair. But I felt nothing. All those years, and I felt absolutely nothing. I was numb. Even at my father's funeral. And I thought that was good."

"Being numb can't feel that good."

"But at least I had dignity."

"Is that what you call shutting everyone out?"

"It's how I survived. I can't apologize for being me. It's the only way I knew how to get through the grief, and the pressure and the unbearable responsibility."

"You have had tremendous pressure," she said. "But you're not alone. You have people who care for you. Deeply."

For a long, agonizing moment there was only silence. Poppy's heart pounded. She felt as if she'd been running a very long, hard race.

His lashes slowly lifted and his light gaze skewered her. "No games," he said quietly.

"No games," she agreed breathlessly.

"Tell me why you came to me tonight. I want the truth."

She couldn't look away from his burning gaze,

couldn't think of anything but him, and wanting him, and needing him and needing to be there for him.

"Don't marry Florrie," she whispered.

And still he said nothing, just looked at her with his intense, penetrating gaze, the one that had always made her feel as if he could see straight through her.

"I don't know if it's too late," she added, breathing in short, shallow, painful gulps of air. "But I want you to have options, and I should be an option. I shouldn't have taken myself off your list. If anyone believes in you, it's me."

"You weren't going to marry without love."

Her eyes burned and the almost overwhelming emotion in her chest put a lump in her throat. "But I'm not marrying without love. We both know I have always loved you."

CHAPTER TEN

POPPY HAD FINISHED dressing an hour ago and was now waiting for Dal to appear. Her gown was quite simply the most beautiful thing she'd ever seen, high necked with a thick gold collar and then gold starburst embellishments and embroidery down the bodice. The long, wide sleeves reminded her of a royal cape, and the soft silk and chiffon dress was fitted through the hips, the skirt straight and sleek, making her feel like a queen. There was more of the exquisite gold starbursts down the front of each sleeve.

Her hair had been pinned up with gold strands twisted in the loose curls. Her hair glittered, and heavy gold diamond earrings swung from her ears.

Looking in the mirror, she didn't even know who she was anymore.

Poppy turned away from her reflection, uneasy with her image. She didn't feel beautiful or regal, and yet the woman in white and gold looked every inch a princess.

How had this happened? How had any of this happened?

If she didn't love Dal so much, she'd pack her bags and run. She didn't know where she'd go, only that she was terrified of losing herself.

Poppy tried not to pace her private courtyard, but it was hard to just sit still when she felt wound so tight.

It had been three days since she'd agreed to marry him, and since then she'd been filled with anxiety and excitement, hope and dread.

She loved him, yes, but at the same time she feared a future where she'd give, give, give and he'd...what?

Would he ever love her? Would attraction and physical desire be enough?

Hopefully, making love would give her the closeness she craved, but not knowing made everything harder.

She couldn't help thinking that it would have been better if they'd made love before today. It would have been better to know more before the ceremony, just so she'd know how to manage her heart.

The wedding was a very simple service. There was no music or fanfare. There was little but the ring ceremony and exchanging of vows.

The paperwork that followed took far more time than the ceremony.

Poppy felt painfully overdressed for such a business-like ceremony. She told herself that she wouldn't cry, and so she didn't cry. It was her own fault for having any sort of expectations in the first place.

Dal had never said he cared for her. Today's ceremony was about convenience, and the brevity of the ceremony reflected the business nature of their union.

This was strictly business.

He'd married her because he'd run out of time. He'd married her to keep his title and lands.

And she? She'd agreed because she hadn't wanted

to lose him. And yet, she'd never had him; at least, she didn't have what she wanted from him. His heart. His love.

His gaze narrowed on her face. "From your expression you'd think we had just attended a funeral instead of a wedding."

"I'm sorry. I'll try to look more celebratory. And maybe I will feel more celebratory once all the paperwork is finished."

"There is always paperwork after a wedding."

"But my impression is that there is considerable more after ours."

"You agreed to this, Poppy. You understood what we were doing today."

"Yes, I did agree. But I could have done this in T-shirt and jeans. I would have probably been happier in a T-shirt and jeans. I know Izba wanted me to look attractive for you, but the dress, shoes and jewelry was overkill."

"She dressed you as if we were marrying at the palace in Gila."

"I wish you had spoken to her."

"I did. I asked her to help you get ready. If you don't like the dress, blame me. I suggested it. It was my mother's wedding dress. The earrings were my mother's, too."

Poppy felt awful. Her eyes suddenly stung and she pressed her nails to her palms. "I didn't know."

"We could have married in Gila. The palace is impressive. There would have been a great deal of pomp and fuss. My family would have preferred we hold the ceremony there, but I didn't want to make this about the family. I wanted this to be about us. I wanted to spend the day with you. After the circus of Langston House, I thought you'd agree. I realize now I was wrong."

"You married me because you had no other choice."

"I married you because you were my first choice."

She bit into her lower lip to keep it from trembling. "You don't have to try to make me feel better—"

"Open and honest communication, remember? I'm telling you the truth. Whether or not you want to believe me is up to you."

It seemed impossible that he would actually want her. She had worked closely with him all these years and he had never been anything but professional and polite. She'd been the one to have feelings for him, not the other way around. But in the end, it didn't really matter about first choice or third choice; hierarchies and rankings were insignificant now that they exchanged their vows and signed the paperwork. They were married. He was her husband and she his wife and he'd fulfilled the terms of the trust with a week to spare.

"Now what?" she asked him. "A game of pool or ping-pong? Or are you going to get back to work?"

He regarded her steadily for a moment before smiling. "You are really upset."

"Yes, I am, and you can turn it into a joke but—"

He silenced her by taking her in his arms, his mouth covering hers. Heat surged through her, heat and longing, the longing so intense that it made her heart ache.

She'd wanted him forever and she'd married him to protect him, but in marrying him, she'd left herself so vulnerable.

He would have access to all of her now—not just

her mind and emotions, but her body. And while she craved his touch, she feared it, too. She feared that once he took her to his bed, he'd see the side of her that she worked so hard to hide.

That she was afraid she wasn't enough.

That she was afraid she'd disappoint him.

That she was afraid he'd regret marrying her when he could have married almost any other woman in the world.

"Stop thinking," he murmured against his mouth, pulling her even closer to him, his hand sliding down her back, a caress to soothe, but the caress inflamed as his palm slid over her rump.

The heat in her veins made her sensitive everywhere, and as he stroked her hip, his tongue parted her lips, claiming her mouth with an urgency that she felt all the way through. Her belly clenched and her thighs trembled and she leaned into him, aroused, so aroused, and yet also so worried that she wouldn't keep his interest.

Little kept the Earl of Langston's interest.

Tears filled her eyes, slipping beneath her closed lashes.

Dal lifted his head, brow furrowing as he stroked her damp cheek. "Why the tears, my watering pot?"

She sniffed and tried to smile, but failed. "I have so many emotions and they're not listening to me today."

He gently wiped away the second tear. A glint of humor warmed his golden eyes. "I don't think your emotions ever listen to you. They're not very obedient, I'm afraid."

He elicited a smile, and her lips wobbled but it was a real smile. "You're making me laugh."

"As if laughter is tragic."

She felt another bubble of reluctant laughter. "Why aren't you falling apart?"

"Because it'd be unmanly to cry on my wedding day."

Poppy snorted.

He smiled down at her. "That's better. No more tears. Izba won't forgive me if we ruin your makeup before the *zaffa*."

"*Zaffa?* What is that?"

"It's the wedding ma—" He broke off at the distant sound of drums.

Poppy stilled, listening to the drums. They were loud and growing louder, and then it wasn't just drums but bagpipes and horns.

She looked up at Dal, confused. "Wedding what?"

"Wedding march." He smiled into her eyes. "I hope you weren't expecting an exciting game of ping-pong, because the festivities are just beginning. After the *zaffa* there will be a party and dinner. It could be a late night."

Somehow Dal had managed to get fifty of his closest Mehkar family members to the Kasbah without her knowing.

She found out later that he'd had them flown to a nearby town and then they had bused in. He had also bused in the musicians and belly dancers and the fierce-looking men carrying flaming swords.

While she'd been dressing and having her hair and makeup done, dozens of Dal's staff had transformed the huge lawn into the site for the Arabic wedding and party. The *zaffa* swept them from the house, down the external stairs, to the grounds below. There was another ceremony after the noisy, colorful, chaotic march. Dal and Poppy had been led up an elevated platform, or *kosha*, to two plush, decorated chairs. Once seated, glasses were passed to all the guests and everyone toasted them, drinking to their health.

After the toast, the royal family's Iman spoke to them about the importance of honoring and respecting each other, and then she and Dal switched rings from their right hand to the left index finger before they were pulled to their feet to dance their first dance ever When the band struck up the second song, the dance floor filled with Dal's family.

Poppy was introduced to so many people, and pulled into so many hugs and kisses, she couldn't keep the guests straight, although Poppy remembered two—the cousin who'd greeted Dal at the Gila airport, and then the tall, somber patriarch of the family, Dal's grand-father, the King of Mehkar.

She'd dropped to a deep curtsy before the king, un-familiar with proper protocol but also profoundly hon-ored that the king would choose to join them today. It couldn't have been an easy trip for a man in his mid-to late-eighties.

The king drew her to her feet, and then lifted her face to his to scrutinize her thoroughly. She blushed beneath his careful inspection, even as it crossed her mind that the king had the same beautiful golden eyes that Dal did.

Dal, she thought, would look like this when he was older, and suddenly she couldn't help but smile at the king.

Dal's grandfather's stern expression eased, and while he didn't quite smile at her, there was warmth and kindness in his eyes as he murmured words in Arabic before kissing each of her cheeks.

"My grandfather welcomes you to the family. He said you will bring us many blessings and much joy."

And then the king moved away and the dancing continued, only interrupted for the cutting of the cake and then again when Dal invited his family and guests to the supper.

It was later in the evening when Dal took her hand and lifted it to his mouth, kissing her fingers. "In our culture the bride and groom always leave before the guests. It is their job to continue the party for us."

And then just like that, they were walking away, hand in hand, as the assembled guests cheered and the drummers drummed and the horns sounded.

A lump filled Poppy's throat at the joyous noise. She glanced back over her shoulder and blinked, not wanting Dal to see that she was crying again on their wedding day. "That was amazing," she whispered. "Beyond anything I could have imagined." She looked up at him and then away, eyes still stinging with tears. "Thank you."

His fingers tightened around hers. "You didn't think I would let our day go without a celebration?"

"I don't know. Maybe I did."

He stopped her then, on the stairs in the shadows, and drew her into his arms for a slow, bone-melting kiss. A shiver of pleasure coursed through her as heat and desire filled her, the warmth sapping her strength so that when his tongue stroked the seam of her lips, she felt weak and breathless. Senses flooded, she opened her mouth to him, giving herself to him, want-

ing to feel everything she could possibly feel on such
a beautiful night.

Below them, laughter and music rose up from the
garden where the band continued to play and Dal's
family talked and danced inside the colorful tents. And
then far above their heads came a crackle and pop, and
then another loud pop and fizz.

Poppy opened her eyes to see fireworks fill the dark
sky with brilliant crimson and gold, green and silver
light. The inky sky came alive with the shooting, ex-
ploding sparkling light.

Poppy's breath caught at the unexpected beauty. But
then everything about today was unexpected. The simple, practical civil ceremony this afternoon, followed
by the exotic, thrilling Arab ceremony and party and
now this: gorgeous, spectacular fireworks. She absolutely adored fireworks, too.

"Is this another tradition in your culture?" she
asked, gaze riveted to the brilliant display above them.

"No. It's something I did for you. You once told me
fireworks made you happy. I wanted you to feel happy."

Her eyes burned and her throat ached, a lump making it impossible to speak. All she could do was nod
and blink and try to keep from falling apart.

He'd thought of her. He'd wanted her happy. Even
though he didn't say the words she wanted to hear, he'd
tried to make today special for her.

"Thank you," she whispered, standing on tiptoe to
kiss him before turning in his arms to watch the fireworks shoot into the sky and explode.

When it was all over, the guests gathered on the
lawn cheered and Poppy applauded and Dal grinned,

looking handsome and boyish and impossibly pleased with himself.

He should be, she thought, running up the stairs with him, heading now for his room, which he'd told her would be their room. He stopped her on the terrace before they reached the tall glass doors, and picked her up, swinging her into his arms, carrying her over the threshold into his darkened bedroom, which had been filled with dozens of flickering candles.

Dal could feel Poppy stiffen as he carried her into the bedroom, her heart racing so hard he could feel it pounding in her rib cage.

"Don't be scared," he said, placing her on her feet. "Nothing terrible is going to happen."

He saw her nervous glance at the bed and he reached out to stroke her warm, flushed cheek. "That won't be terrible, either, but we're not going to bed yet. I thought we should change and have some champagne and dessert. We left the party before the dessert was served."

She gave a half nod, her expression still wary. He didn't blame her. It had been an overwhelming day and he'd known what would happen today.

He'd kept the *zaffa* and party secret from her, wanting to surprise her, but maybe it would have been better to let her in on the plans so that she wouldn't have been so sad earlier after the civil ceremony. He'd hated the shadows that had darkened her eyes when she'd thought the civil ceremony was all that had been planned. It had made him realize how sensitive she really was, and how much she'd need emotionally. But that would be the problem.

He could give her things, and place credit cards

without limits in her hands, but he'd never give her the intimacy and emotional closeness she craved, but God help him, he would try.

"I'll open the champagne while you change," he said. "I believe Izba is waiting in the bedroom to help you out of your bridal gown and into a more comfortable dressing gown."

Dressing gown was overstating things, Poppy thought, inspecting herself in the mirror. Dressing gown implied weight and coverage, but this sheer ivory kaftan with the scattered circles of diamonds and gold beads hid nothing. Oh, there was fabric all right; the gown was wildly romantic with shirred shoulders and a plunging neckline that went nearly down to her waist, but if it wasn't for the strategic draping Dal would be able to see absolutely everything.

As it was she had a hard time keeping her nipples from popping through the fabric, never mind the dark curls at the apex of her thighs.

"Izba, I can't go to him like this," Poppy muttered, blushing. "I'm practically naked."

"It's your wedding night," Izba answered soothingly. "And you look so beautiful."

"Beautifully naked." She frowned as she walked, aware that any light shining behind her would give away everything. "Was this another of his mother's gowns?"

"No. His Highness brought this one back from Gila for you. It was custom made." She gave Poppy a pat on the back. "Go to him. Don't be shy. He loves you very much—"

"He doesn't love me, Izba."

"Nonsense."

"He doesn't. He told me so." Poppy's voice suddenly broke. "But I knew it. I've known it. And I'm not going to cry about it. I'm not crying today."

"He wouldn't marry you if he didn't love you."

"He married me because he *had* to be married. He needed a wife by his thirty-fifth birthday."

"His Highness can have any woman. Many women would marry him. But you are the one he wanted."

Poppy wanted to explain that he hadn't had real choices, nor the time to explore all his options. Sophie disappearing from Langston Chapel had put him in a bind, and so Dal had settled...he'd settled for her. "It's more complicated than that," she said faintly. "His Highness had tremendous pressure on him—"

"Stop making excuses for him. He's a man. And he wouldn't have married you if this isn't what he wanted, not just for him, but also, to be the mother of his children."

The ever-important heirs and spares, Poppy thought with a panicked gulp.

She shot Izba a quick, nervous smile and then exited the bedroom before she lost her courage altogether.

Dal had dimmed the lights while she was gone, and he was waiting for her on his grand terrace. He gestured for her to come to him and she hesitated, suddenly shy, aware that she was next to naked.

His gaze met hers and held.

He gestured again, a masculine gesture of power and ownership.

She didn't want to go to him, but at the same time, she couldn't resist. She walked slowly, self-consciously, aware of the way he watched her, a hot, possessive light heating the gold of his eyes.

The soft chiffon and silk gown floated around her ankles as she crossed the floor. Izba had unpinned her hair, taking out the gold beads, and she could feel her hair brushing her shoulders.

"Why are you looking at me like that?" she breathed.

"Because you're gorgeous and you're mine."

Her tummy did a flip. "I think I need that champagne."

He carried their glasses to the low couch and sat down. He placed one glass on the table and then patted the cushion next to him with his free hand. "I have your glass here. You just have to come to me to get it."

"You like being in control, don't you?"

The corner of his mouth lifted. "No. I love being in control."

"So what are your plans for me?"

"Come here, and I'll tell you."

It seemed like it took her forever to reach his side, but at last she was there, heart racing, her mouth so dry. As she carefully sat down next to him she held out her hand for the champagne. He handed her the flute and she took a hasty sip, the cold, tart bubbles warming and fizzing all the way down. She took another sip for courage and then another to help her relax.

Dal reached out and removed the glass from her trembling fingers. "Easy," he cautioned. "You don't want to get sick."

"It's just champagne."

"Exactly."

She drew a quick breath, wondering how this would go, and what it'd be like to consummate the marriage. "You said it will sting."

"It's what I've been told."

"Will it be bad?"

He reached out and pushed her heavy hair back from her face. "I am not an expert in virgins. The whole idea of deflowering a woman has never appealed to me."

"I thought men loved the idea of being the first."

"I think those must be very insecure men."

"You wouldn't care if I'd been with other men?"

"Do you care that I've been with other women?"

"Yes."

His eyes flashed fire, and his head dropped, his mouth covering hers. The kiss was hot and slow, and so incredibly sensual it made her head spin.

She reached for him, holding on to his shoulders, pulling herself closer, needing more of his warmth, and strength and skin. She remembered the night in the pool and how he'd felt against her, and she wanted that pressure and pleasure now.

"Please take your shirt off," she murmured. "Let me feel you."

"If you want it off, you take it off," he answered, his deep voice pitched low.

She felt a frisson of nervous excitement at the hungry, predatory gleam in his eyes as she rose up on her knees to better reach the middle button on his shirt since the top ones were already undone.

When she struggled to get the button unfastened he lifted her off her knees and placed her on his lap, so that she was straddling him, her sheer gown floating out on either side as if they were wings of a jeweled butterfly. Poppy could feel the hard press of his arousal through his trousers. She was wearing nothing beneath her delicate gown and his thick, blunt head pressed against her core.

He was hard, and hot and she shuddered as he shifted his hips, his length rubbing against her where she was open and sensitive.

"My shirt?" he drawled, leaning back to watch her at her task.

Her hands shook as she struggled to unfasten one button and then another. Again, he shifted his hips, the rocking motion deliberate, and this time she pressed down on him, welcoming the feel of his thick tip pressing between her folds, nudging her bud, flooding her with pleasure.

Poppy glanced up into his face. His black lashes had dropped over his eyes, concealing his expression, and yet the sensual set of his full, firm mouth sent twin shots of lust and adrenaline through her.

He was so beautiful. So incredibly handsome and physical.

She'd never met any man half so appealing. Had never met any man she'd wanted the way she wanted him. She'd fought her attraction for years, but there was no more fighting her desire, or him. She just wanted to be his. She wanted to belong to him.

"Are we going to just leave the shirt on?" he asked, arching a brow. He didn't sound annoyed, or impatient. If anything, he sounded very pleased with himself, and her and all of this.

"Focusing now," she answered, forcing herself to finish with the unbuttoning of the shirt, even though she could barely focus thanks to the heat of his thighs and the way the hard length of him seemed to be making her melt.

And then at last his shirt was open and she leaned forward, her breasts brushing his chest, to push the smooth fabric off his shoulders and then down each arm until his arms were free and his muscular torso was beautifully bare. Her breasts brushed against him again as she reached for the shirt and tossed it away.

"You are a tease," he growled.

"Me? You're the one making me do all the work," she answered, even as she flashed him a shy, breathless smile.

The air practically crackled and hummed with desire. Dal had to fight to keep his hands at his sides and not touch Poppy as she finished stripping the shirt off his arms.

Her full breasts had swayed and bounced beneath the sheer ivory chiffon fabric, her dark pink nipples teasing the hell out of him, the tips pebbled tight. It didn't help that she was impossibly hot and wet. He wanted to bury himself inside her, thrusting hard and deep, but she was inexperienced and even though it had been years since he'd made love, he wasn't going to rush their first night. He wanted her to see herself as he saw her—seductive, stunning, powerful, feminine. Perfect.

He reached up to touch her, finding her breast through her sheer beaded gown. Her nipple puckered tighter at the touch and she gasped a little as he pinched the tender peak. He watched her face as he stroked her and then took her breast into his mouth.

She groaned as he sucked and kneaded the warm, sensitive peak with his tongue and lips. He reached up to cup her other breast while he continued sucking. She rocked against him, hot and damp and aching for relief, and it crossed his mind that he'd never seen anything half as erotic as Poppy rocking on his lap.

He wanted so badly to be inside her. He wanted to feel her tight heat wrap his length, and when his control threatened to snap, he swung her into his arms and carried her into the bedroom, placing her in the middle of the bed.

She fell backward with a soft sigh onto the sheets. She was still breathing hard, her beautiful, dark eyes wide and luminous, her cheeks flushed, her luscious lips parted and pink. He leaned over her, drinking her in, thinking she was the most beautiful woman he'd ever known.

Poppy.

His wife.

His pleasure.

Poppy reached for him, bringing his head down to hers so he'd kiss her again. She loved the way he kissed. She loved the way he touched her. He was touching her now, caressing her breast through the filmy gown and then lower, stroking her flat stomach, across her hip and down the outside of her thigh.

Her legs trembled as he slid his hand between her thighs, parting them.

"Don't be nervous," he said.

"I'm not," she lied.

He dipped his head to hers, his mouth covering hers in a slow, hot, dizzying kiss. She relaxed as he caressed the inside of her thigh, stroking down to the back of her knee, and then up again.

She could feel his fingers trailing over the inside of her thigh again, so very close that his knuckles brushed her dark curls. Her breath caught as his knuckles lightly trailed across her mound, the light, teasing caress sliding the delicate gown across her, as well.

She was ready to have his hands on her, skin against skin, ready to feel him touch her as he had in the pool, with his clever expert fingers against her where she was aching and wet.

"You're torturing me," she complained when his knuckles brushed over her again, the sensation too light to bring relief and yet too firm to be ignored.

"I don't want to rush you."

"I've been aroused for hours."

"Not hours," he answered, his fingertips trailing over her, pressing the now beaded chiffon over her tender folds and then holding it against her core. "Maybe a half hour."

She felt herself throbbing as he cupped her, his palm capturing her heat and dampness. She could feel her moisture on his hand.

Dal reached for the filmy hem of her gown and lifted it up, drawing it up over her knees, and then her thighs and then over her head, leaving her naked.

She felt his gaze as it took her in. He was studying her so intently she felt as if he was memorizing her. And then his hand returned to her knee, skimming down her shin to her ankle, and then back over her calf.

He caressed her leg until she relaxed and he opened her legs wider, and leaning over her hips, he placed at kiss just above her pelvic bone, and then another one lower, in the middle of her curls.

She shivered at the warmth of his breath and then shivered again when he parted her curls, exposing her tender skin and slick inner folds before placing a kiss right to the heart of her.

His mouth felt cool where she burned, his tongue flicking her and curling around her, toying with the delicate skin, stirring every nerve, making her feel wanton and desperate and yet also empty.

She reached for his belt, tugging it free. He lifted his head, and she nodded. "Please lose the trousers."

He did, very quickly, and with the trousers removed his heavy shaft sprang free.

"I don't think that will fit," she said hoarsely.

"It will. You'll see," he answered, lowering himself over her, kissing her, his tongue stroking the seam of her lips and then the inside of her mouth before catching the tip of her tongue, making her squirm.

With his knee he pressed her legs apart, making room to settle his hips between her thighs. She felt his shaft rub against her as he positioned himself near her core, the tip gliding across her wet entrance, making her feel delicious things.

He didn't try to enter her, instead focusing on kissing and touching her neck, her earlobe, the sensitive skin beneath her breast. She liked the feel of his strong thighs between hers, his legs hard with muscle and slightly rough with hair. Little by little his powerful thighs opened her wider, and the smooth, thick head of his shaft settled at her core, pressing in.

Dal lifted his head. "Look at me," he said quietly. "It's just me and you, and it will only sting this once."

And then he was pressing into her, a slow, steady thrust that made her eyes water and her breath catch, from the fullness and pressure of him filling her. It was a lot of sensation. It felt like too much sensation. The stretching was no longer remotely comfortable.

"Breathe," he murmured, kissing her lips. "That's it, breathe."

As she breathed in, he thrust deeper, breaking through the resistance. It hurt. It did. She blinked rapidly at the burn, and then the strange fullness of him lodged so deep inside her.

It wasn't what she'd imagined.

It was more than she'd imagined.

More pressure, more warmth, more fullness, more pain.

"Breathe," he said again.

She struggled to smile. "Don't worry, I'm not going to faint."

"It will feel better when I move. Let me move. It'll help ease the tightness."

"If I didn't like you so much I'd hate you."

He kissed the corner of her lips, and then her full lower lip, and then pressing up so that his weight was on his arms, he pulled out of her and then gently thrust back in. He did it again, and then again, and he was right; she wasn't as uncomfortable anymore. In fact, as he moved she began to feel something that rather resembled pleasure.

She closed her eyes to concentrate on the sensation and yes, it was a nice sensation, better then nice, as with each of Dal's deep, slow thrusts she felt heat grow and sensation coil, and she reached for him, hands sliding up his lean chiseled torso, fingers spreading wide across his warm satin skin. She could feel the hard, taut muscles beneath his skin and the way they tightened with every thrust of his hips.

Every time he buried himself in her, he stroked a sensitive spot inside, and it made her breath catch and want to press up against him to hold him there. "Yes," he said hoarsely, "just like that," as she rocked her hips again.

The next time he stroked down into her she rocked up and the pleasure was even more intense. She clenched him with her inner muscles, trying to hold him. He growled with pleasure. Poppy felt a thrill like nothing she'd ever felt better.

It was, she thought, rather amazing how their bodies came together, his hardness buried deep in her wet, slick heat, and this simple joining could make her never want to let him go. She wrapped her arms around him, holding tighter, his tempo quickening, stroking her faster and harder. The feel of him in her was maddening and delicious. Her body burned and glowed and she arched up as he pressed deep, her heels digging into the bed to give herself traction.

"Can you come?" he asked.

"I don't know," she said, because there was so much pressure and tension and desire but she couldn't focus on anything but the hard, silky feel of him filling her.

Suddenly, his hand was there between their bodies, and his fingers found her nub and he stroked the sensitive spot as he thrust deeply. The sensation felt so perfect; everything about this was perfect, and as he filled her and touched her, she felt overwhelming love.

He was everything to her. He was the very center of her world.

His deep thrusts were sending her over the edge. She

couldn't fight the building sensation anymore. With a cry, she shattered, the climax stunning and intense. He thrust into her one more time, burying himself so deeply that she felt his muscles tighten and contract as his orgasm followed hers.

For several moments after, Poppy didn't know where she was, or who she was. She'd felt thrown to the stars and she'd somehow floated back.

Slowly, reality returned and she turned her head to look at Dal, who was lying on his back next to her.

He was the most beautiful person in the world. There was no one more dear or special to her.

Her eyes filled with tears. She blinked hard, trying to keep them from falling. "I love you," she whispered. "I love you so much it hurts my heart."

He gazed back at her, his golden gaze shuttered.

She held her breath, waiting to hear what he would say. But he just looked at her for a long moment, then leaned over, kissed her. "I hope today was special."

"It was," she answered, trying not to feel empty after feeling so incredibly much. He wasn't being cold, she told herself. This was just him. Dal wasn't good at expressing emotion. He'd never say the words she wanted to hear. "It was magical."

He kissed her again and pulled her close to his side and he was soon asleep. Exhausted, Poppy lay next to him, emotions unhinged, thoughts racing, still too wound up to sleep.

Everything had changed in one day.

She'd done what she'd intended to do. She'd protected Dal, but she'd left herself completely open and vulnerable.

This life with Dal would not be easy on her heart.

* * *

Sunlight pierced the gap between the heavy drapes that had been drawn across the windows. Poppy rolled onto her back, stretching and yawning.

She winced a little as she rolled onto her back, feeling a new soreness between her thighs. She flashed back to the intense lovemaking and blushed, remembering his mouth and lips on her, exploring her, and then the way he'd filled her, burying himself in her, making her feel more connected to him than she'd ever been with anyone.

Poppy reached out to see if Dal was still with her, but he was gone.

She turned to look at the place he should have been, and could still see an indentation from his big frame.

She stroked the sheet in his spot. It was cool. He'd been gone a long time.

Poppy slowly sat up, drawing the covers with her. Last night had been a revelation. She hadn't expected the closeness, nor had she realized that a man's body could feel like that…the sinewy pressure of Dal's thighs, and the warm, hard planes of his chest. She could still remember how she'd clung to him, arms wrapped tightly, feeling as if she'd never get close enough. Poppy didn't know if this was how everyone felt when they made love, but the intensity of it had been shattering. She'd anticipated pleasure, and she'd expected new sensations, but she hadn't expected that the desire would become pure emotion.

When he'd filled her, and held her and thrust so deeply into her, she'd wanted to burst out of her skin and crawl into his.

She wanted him, all of him, his mind, body and soul.

It was why she'd told him she loved him. She wanted to be part of his heart, and safe in his heart and feel secure forever.

But she didn't feel secure.

If anything, making love had made her feel more alone and isolated than before.

It was late afternoon before Poppy saw Dal. He found her down by the pool, reading beneath an umbrella. He leaned over her, kissed her and then sat down on the chair, apologizing for being gone all day, explaining that he'd spent much of the day making sure his family returned safely to Gila, and then a problem had come up in the London office and he'd been on conference calls ever since.

It wasn't until he sat down next to her that she realized he was wearing the traditional white robe of his people.

"Where has Randall Grant gone?" she asked, and she wasn't just referring to the clean, elegant lines of the robe, but the gradual transformation that had taken place since they flew out of Winchester. In England he'd been so private and contained. He wasn't just more open here; his personality was warmer, too. He smiled here, and made jokes and teased her. And made love to her. Her cheeks heated remembering last night.

"Do you want him back?"

"Not necessarily. Although he is the you I know best."

"There is just one of me. But the me here is more relaxed. Happier, too," he added, leaning forward to kiss her, a hot, erotic kiss that made her tummy tighten and her breasts peak. She was breathless when he pulled away.

"Are you happy here?" he added.

"It's beautiful but very remote."

He studied her face for a moment. "Was it not a good day?"

"It was a rather long day. I got lonely."

"I'm sorry. I expected to be free sooner." He pressed another lingering kiss to her lips before rising. "I'm going to go shower and change. Join me soon. I've asked for some drinks and a light meal to be sent to our room since I haven't eaten anything today."

She reached for his hand, catching his fingers, preventing him from leaving. "What's happening at the office?"

"A problem, not an emergency. Nothing you need to worry about."

"Is there anything I can do?"

He squeezed her hand and then let it go. "I have one of the administrative assistants in the office taking care of some things for me and soon we'll have your replacement. It's just a temporary stress, nothing to trouble you."

And then he was gone, striding toward the Kasbah, his long white robe swirling, reminding her of a powerful desert warlord just returning home while she very much felt like a concubine with no purpose other than being available to please her master.

She grimaced, frustrated, not wanting to be shut out from his life, or his business. She'd worked with him for years and had enjoyed the partnership. What were her responsibilities in this new role of hers?

Poppy pushed off the chair and went to her room to shower and change before going on upstairs.

"Where did you change?" Dal asked her when she entered his suite of rooms.

"My room."

"This is your room now," he said. "I expected you would have the staff move your things today."

"You never said anything."

"You are my wife. This is the master bedroom suite. This is where you belong."

"How do I know if you don't tell me?"

"I'm telling you now."

Poppy compressed her lips, not liking his autocratic tone. "This is all new to me, Dal. You're going to have to communicate a little bit."

"You're upset with me?"

She fought to keep her voice steady, not wanting to sound hysterical on their second day of married life. "You were gone when I woke up. You didn't leave a note, or tell me when you'd return."

"I didn't know myself."

"In England you communicated far better."

"In England you were my secretary."

"Maybe I liked being your secretary better than your wife!"

He gave her an intense, brooding look. "Really?"

Her pulse quickened, her chest tightening. "I don't want to be shut out of your life."

"You're not. You are the very center of my world now." And then as if to prove his point, he swept her into his arms, carrying her to the bed where he tossed her, pinned her down and kissed her fiercely, deeply, the scorching kiss torching her senses.

As he kissed her, he slid a hand between her legs, caressing her thighs until she opened them for him. He leaned over and kissed the top of her thigh, and then the inside of her thigh and she trembled.

"I'm not sure I can handle *this*," she murmured unsteadily as she felt his fingers slide over her, lightly tracing her folds and then lightly, lightly parting her before placing a kiss on her, and then another kiss, followed by a flick of his tongue across her clit.

She gasped as sharp, delicious sensation shot through her and when he covered her there with his mouth and sucked, her hips jerked up of their own accord. Dal shifted his weight, clamped an arm across her pelvis, holding her open and still while he kissed, sucked and licked her to an orgasm so powerful she dug her nails into his shoulders and screamed his name.

The orgasm was so intense she felt almost broken. The intensity of the sensation made her feel emotional and undone. Flushed, spent, she felt him stretch out next to her and pull her to his side. He left his arm around her, his palm covering her breast.

"I want to be in you," he said, "but I don't want to hurt you. Maybe tomorrow."

She nodded, glad he couldn't see the tears filling her eyes.

She hadn't thought sex would feel like this…physical and carnal but then afterward, painfully empty.

It was hard to love someone who didn't love you back.

"Poppy?" he asked, shifting her so that she lay on her back. He pushed her thick hair from her face and then untangled a strand still clinging to her damp cheek. "What's wrong?"

"Nothing."

"Something is. You're far too quiet."

She looked up at him, seeing his strong brow and the high, hard lines of his cheekbones. She loved his face. It was so very beautiful and familiar. But the rest of this…it was new and overwhelming. In bed, he was overwhelming. The sex was overwhelming. His body was so big, and powerful and sexual. He was so very sexual. But then after all the physical intimacy there was no emotional intimacy. If anything, after sex, she felt even further from him than before.

"Is this what you thought marriage would be like?" she asked carefully.

"No. It's better." He smiled crookedly. "You're not just my friend, but now you're my lover."

"So you're satisfied? Happy you married me?"

"No regrets." He rolled onto his back and pulled her toward him so that she was lying against his side, her cheek on his chest. "And you? Regrets, my sweet Poppy?"

It took her a moment to answer. "No regrets," she said unsteadily. "But I think I may be a little homesick. We've been gone a long time."

His hand stroked her hair and then trailed down her spine. "What do you miss most? Winchester? London?"

"My flat."

His hand stilled in the small of her back. "Why your flat?"

"It was cozy and familiar. I felt…safe…there."

"But Poppy, your home is with me now. I have promised to take care of you, and I will. You must know you are safe with me."

She nodded, eyes closing, holding back the hot emotion, because despite his words, she didn't feel safe. She didn't feel secure. She didn't have what she needed—love.

Sex was good and fine, and pleasure was definitely nice, but what she needed most in the world was to be truly needed, to be truly special, to be truly loved.

CHAPTER ELEVEN

THEY FELL INTO a pattern over the next week, a pattern Poppy did not enjoy. Dal would be sequestered in his office working while she drifted around the Kasbah trying to find ways to occupy herself. She'd asked if she could work with him, or assist him like she used to, but he curtly reminded her she was his wife now, not an employee.

After that he seemed to withdraw even more, at least during the day when he was distant and unavailable. But then in the evening he emerged from his office and was warm and charming and always he'd make love to her. The sex was incredibly hot, and he never failed to make sure she climaxed, but the long days of being alone followed by the carnal lovemaking was breaking her heart.

He'd take her body, and pleasure her body, but that was all he wanted from her.

And that was also all he'd give her.

"We will leave here soon for Gila," he said on the ninth night of their honeymoon, in that quiet aftermath that followed their lovemaking. "I thought perhaps we could look for our home in Gila together. Would you enjoy that?"

Her brow creased. "Are we going to live in Gila?"

"I'd like to have a home in the capital. Maybe something modern, or if you prefer classical architecture—"

"What about England? What about our home there?"

"My intention is to divide our time between the two. I want my children to know Mehkar and be comfortable in both places."

"They would be my children, too," she said in a small voice.

"Of course. I meant our children."

She wasn't so sure he did.

Poppy couldn't sleep that night, but she didn't lie awake tossing and turning. No, she spent the long, quiet hours of the night making a brutal but necessary decision.

She'd given Dal what he'd needed. She'd protected his lands and title. But now it was time she protected herself.

In the morning she would leave, and she wouldn't go in tears. She was going to leave strong and proud and focused on her future for a change, not his.

He was at his desk when she entered his office. He didn't even look up for a minute, so engrossed in the document he was reading.

She watched him read, feeling a pang of love and regret, recognizing the Randall Grant focus.

No one could compartmentalize like Dal.

She shifted the hands holding her purse and worn travel bag but made no other sound. Finally, he glanced up at her, his strong black brows flattening over his light eyes.

"What's happening?" he said brusquely.

She didn't take offense. She knew it was his tone when concentrating. His sharpness wasn't aimed at her but rather the annoyance of breaking his focus. He wouldn't like what she had to say, but it was time, and she'd made her mind up. "I'd like to leave now."

For a moment there was just silence and then he slowly rose. "What did you say?"

"You told me when you found a new secretary, you'd put me on a plane. You have a new secretary. I know she's working in the London office right now, but she replaced me a week ago."

"You're my wife, Poppy, not an employee."

"Please have your helicopter come and take me to Gila. I intend to sleep tonight in my own bed, at home."

"I don't understand."

"I know you don't, and I don't expect you will, but this marriage helped you, but it's not good for me. Please do the right thing for me, and let me go. If you care for me at all, you'll send me home now."

He moved away from the desk, walking slowly toward her. "I won't send you back to England like this—"

"So you don't care for me."

"I won't send you because I do."

"Then you're not listening. I'm not happy here. I'm not happy living like this. I don't regret marrying you, and I won't call it a mistake, because I gave you what you needed…the title, the house, the estates…so please give me now what I need. My freedom."

Dal was grateful for twenty years of lessons in control and discipline because it allowed him to keep his expression mercifully blank. He was stunned, though. Inwardly reeling.

"I am listening," he said casually, calmly, as he approached her. "I always listen to you, even when you think I'm sleeping. I am there in bed with you, hearing you breathe, hearing you weep—"

"If you've heard me cry at night, why didn't you say something, or do something? Why just let me cry myself to sleep?"

"Marriage is new, and an adjustment. I thought you needed time."

"No, I didn't need time. I needed *you*." She nearly backed up a step as he closed the distance, stopping just a foot in front of her. Her chin lifted, her dark eyes bright with anger and pain. "*You*, Dal," she repeated fiercely, "not time. All I've had here is time."

"But you have me. I sleep with you every night. I hold you through the night. I am not far during the day, and when you need me, you can find me. Just as you found me today."

Silence greeted his words. Her eyes narrowed a fraction and then her lips curved but there was no warmth in her eyes. "This you," she said at last, nodding at him, "the one you're offering, the one you're giving, it's not enough. I'm sorry if it hurts, but it's the truth."

He'd never seen this side of her. He didn't know what to make of her anger. "People are not perfect. They will inevitably let you down. I'm sorry if I've disappointed you—"

"There are small disappointments, life's little irritations and then there are tragedies. I can handle the irritations. I expect the irritations and annoyances. But me marrying a man who doesn't love me…that borders on tragedy."

She'd stunned him again. He couldn't think of a single appropriate thing to say. Poppy, for her part, was so still and pale she reminded him of a wax figure.

"Please put me on the plane—"

"No. Absolutely not."

"So you don't care for me. I am just another of your toys and possessions."

"I don't know where this is coming from, and I don't know what has made you feel so insecure—"

"You have, Dal! You with your lack of words and lack of emotion. You only make room for me in bed. But out of bed, there is no place for me in your life!"

"You are bordering on hysteria."

"Of course you'll mock me and shame my emotions, but at least I have emotions! At least I feel, and at least I'm able to be honest about what I need. I need a man who will love me. I need a man who will share with me and sacrifice for me." Her voice cracked, broke. "But from the beginning it's been about you, and as long as I stay here, it will only be about you, and I was wrong to think I could do this…live like this. So let me go now while we both have some dignity."

"I'd rather lose my dignity than you."

"You've already lost me."

"No, I haven't. You're hurt and angry, but we can fix this."

"It's impossible to fix us. We can't be fixed. You can't be fixed—"

"I am not a machine! I have feelings—" he broke off, grinding his teeth together, trying to hold the blistering pain. "And maybe it shocks you, but your words hurt. Your words wound. But I'll take the words and the wounds if it will allow us to grow stronger together."

She averted her head, lips quivering. "I don't want us to be together. Not anymore."

"I don't believe you. I can't believe you. After four years—"

"I didn't know the real you! I didn't know us."

He felt like he was in quicksand and sinking fast. Emotions were not his strength. Tears and sadness and grief and need…they baffled him. He'd never been allowed to feel or grieve, and he'd learned to survive by being numb. But he wasn't numb right now. His chest burned. His body hurt. She might as well have poured petrol on him and then struck a match. "Perhaps what you should be saying," he said tightly, "is that you didn't know you."

She looked at him then, tears in her eyes. "But I did know me. I knew what I needed. And every time I refused your proposal it was because I knew what I needed…and that was love."

"Poppy, I am trying, with everything I am——"

"It's not enough." Her chin lifted, eyes glittering with tears. "Call for the helicopter. I'll be downstairs in the garden, waiting."

Poppy walked away then, quickly, her heels clicking on the marble, her eyes scalding.

That was beyond brutal. That was awful, so very awful. She'd said hard, harsh things, not to hurt him, but to make him understand that this wasn't a game. She was done. She felt broken. He had to let her go.

She sat in the garden on a bench waiting for the helicopter, her bags at her feet. She would stay in the garden until the helicopter arrived, too. It might take days, but eventually he'd know she was serious.

Thirty minutes later Dal emerged from the Kasbah with his large black suitcase. She watched him cross the lawn and then he squeezed onto the bench next to her. She refused to make eye contact. This wasn't an act. It wasn't a game. She was leaving him today.

"The helicopter should be here in the next five to ten minutes," he said, breaking the silence.

"Good."

"The jet has been fueled and is ready in Gila."

"Thank you."

"I needed to file a flight plan and I told them London."

"That's correct."

"Good. Glad to know I've done something right."

She shot him a furious glance. "I don't feel sorry for you. You're a grown man, a very successful man. You have extensive experience in mergers and acquisitions. You're accustomed to the bumps and disappointments. You'll bounce back in no time."

He met her gaze and held it. "You're not a merger, or an acquisition. You are my wife, and you're hurt, and I'm sorry. Your happiness means everything to me."

"Those are just words."

"But isn't that what you wanted? Words? Tender words? Affectionate words?"

"You can't even say them!"

"Love, you mean?" His black eyebrow arched. "I do love you, Poppy, and yet I find the word hard to say, but that doesn't mean I don't feel it."

"Huh!"

He caught her jaw, turned her face to him. "I'm not a machine. I feel emotions. In fact, I feel them so intensely they scare me. I have spent my entire life trying to contain my emotions, determined that they wouldn't dictate my future. And every time I said I wanted you, I meant it. I wanted you then, and I want you now."

"Sexually," she said, bitterly.

"Sexually, emotionally, spiritually. I want you as my partner, my best friend—"

"Your *only* friend."

"The mother of my children," he continued calmly.

She gave her head a toss. "For the all-important heirs."

"Not heirs," he corrected, "but us, our family. You'll be an incredible mother. And I'd like to be a father, although I'm not sure I'll be good at it in the beginning. I'll have to learn, but I can."

"You never talked about family before. You and Sophie—"

"Because I couldn't imagine raising a family with Sophie. I couldn't imagine a life with her. But I can with you. I can imagine everything, and I want everything, and I do mean everything. You, Poppy, have made me want more."

She bit her lip and looked away, tears in her eyes. "It's too little, too late, Dal. You've hurt me—"

"I did. I know I did, and I'm sorry. Poppy, I am an arse. I'm ruthless and relentless but none of this should surprise you. You know me. And you married me, knowing me."

"True, and I've realized you haven't changed. You'll never change. I'm not going to change, either. I will always want more and you will want less."

"If I wanted less, why did I marry you? If I wanted less, why didn't I pick one of those silly party girls who would have been grateful for my wealth and position, instead of throwing it in my face? If I wanted less, why did I choose the woman who wanted *more*? Who demands more? Who insists I demand more, too? If less was my future, then why have I struggled to grow and change for you?"

She said nothing.

Frustration filled him. "Poppy, who would I be without you?" And then he fell silent, his question hanging there between them for what felt like forever.

Finally unable to bear the silence a moment longer, she said, "You are the Earl of Langston and the Prince of Mehkar."

"Actually, I'm not the Earl of Langston anymore."

She looked at him, aghast.

He shrugged. "You're not the only one who can make grand gestures. I can, too, and I've chosen to walk away from the title and the house and everything it entails. It was a bit more complicated than I imagined, but it's done now. It's what I've been working on since our wedding."

"The problem in London?"

He nodded.

"But you married me to secure—"

"You. I married you because I couldn't imagine going through life without you. Poppy, I don't care about titles and houses. I don't need anything but you."

"Then why the rush? Why the pressure?"

"I wanted to keep the promise I made to my father. And I did. And now I'm free."

She looked away, blinking back tears.

"I am not good with words, my sweet Poppy, but you are my other half. You are my heart and my soul. You are my family and my future. Please don't leave, and if you're determined to go, then plan on taking me."

She brushed away her tears. "You won't like my crowded, untidy little flat."

"I will if that's where you want to be. If that's what feels like home."

"The flat's so small there's barely room for me, never mind you."

"We'll downsize."

She spluttered on laughter. "You have no idea what you're saying. You're accustomed to huge houses and servants and people bowing and scraping."

"Not anymore. I've given it up."

"What about here in Mehkar? Are you still Prince Talal, or have you dispensed with that, too?"

"No, I'm still Prince Talal." He grimaced. "And I should probably tell you something that I ought to have told you long ago."

"Oh, no." She looked at him, immediately wary. "I don't know if I want to hear this." She looked into his eyes, worried. "What is it? What else have you done?"

"I haven't done anything yet. You see, I am my grandfather's heir. When he dies, I will be king."

"Oh, Dal."

"I know it's a lot to process—"

"He's healthy, though, isn't he? At least he seemed relatively fit and strong when he was here for the wedding."

"He's as healthy as an eighty-four-year-old man can be."

"That's good."

He regarded her a moment, the corners of his mouth curving. "You took that better than I expected."

"You must know I don't really wish to be a queen. I just want a cozy little house in the Cotswolds—"

"With a couch and a telly." He smiled and kissed her. "I promise you'll have the house you've always dreamed about. And the television set, too."

"Are you making fun of me?"

"Absolutely not. I'm just trying to reassure you that I'm listening and attentive to your needs."

She groaned and rolled her eyes. "You are impossible."

"Yes, I know. But isn't that what you always liked about me?"

EPILOGUE

TALAL'S CORONATION WAS nearly ten years to the day of their wedding at Kasbah Jolie.

It was early July and impossibly hot. The Gila palace was air-conditioned but with so many guests crowded into the reception room, the air conditioner couldn't quite do its job.

Poppy was miserable in her gold gown and heels. Not because the kaftan was tight; if anything it was made of the lightest, softest silk imaginable, but she was very pregnant, nine months pregnant, and her ankles were swelling and she was desperate to be off her feet.

Thank goodness she knew what to expect. This was her fourth pregnancy and she always felt irritable at this stage, ready for the bump to be gone and the baby to be in her arms. She was always anxious as the due date grew closer, worried about any number of things that could go wrong. Fortunately, the first three deliveries went without a hitch and all three were really good children, and very excited about the new one, because finally the three boys would have a baby sister.

Poppy struggled to not fidget as Dal accepted his new crown, and the duties it entailed.

But it was hard to stand perfectly still with the odd contractions. They were false contractions, she was sure. She'd had them with the last two pregnancies and she knew now not to be alarmed.

She pressed her elbow to her side, pressing against the tension that wrapped her abdomen.

She must be overly hot and overly tired because that one felt like the real thing.

And then her water broke and Poppy's head jerked up. Dal was suddenly looking at her and she didn't remember speaking, or making a sound, but suddenly he was there, at her side, his arm around her.

"What's happening?"

"My water just broke," she whispered, aware that all two hundred plus people in the reception room were watching. "But it's too early. She's not due for another couple of weeks."

"Apparently, no one told her that," he said, smiling warmly into her eyes.

Poppy's heart turned over. Ten years of marriage and he still made her melt. "I'm sorry we're disrupting the ceremony."

"I'm not. I can't wait to meet her. You know how much I've wanted a daughter."

Another contraction hit and Poppy gasped and squeezed his arm. "It seems she's in a rush to meet you, too!"

"I'm not surprised. If she's anything like her mother, she's going to be fierce and loyal and impossibly loving." He wrapped his arm around her waist, supporting her. "I love you, Queen Poppy, completely and madly, you know."

"What has happened to my safe, predictable Englishman?"

"Gone, I'm afraid."

She gripped his arm as another contraction hit.

"And so are we," he added, swinging her into his arms. "Because I don't trust our little princess not to make an appearance here and now."

* * * * *

If you enjoyed
KIDNAPPED FOR HIS ROYAL DUTY
by Jane Porter,
look out for Caitlin Crews's
contribution to their STOLEN BRIDES *duet*

THE BRIDE'S BABY OF SHAME

Available July 2018!

And in the meantime,
why not explore these other stories by Jane Porter?

HIS MERCILESS MARRIAGE BARGAIN
HER SINFUL SECRET
BOUGHT TO CARRY HIS HEIR

Available now!

#3637 HIS MILLION-DOLLAR MARRIAGE PROPOSAL
The Powerful Di Fiore Tycoons
by Jennifer Hayward

Lazzero needs a fake fiancée to win a business deal. He offers to absolve Chiara's father's bankruptcy, *if* she wears his ring! But with their explosive attraction, soon Lazzero wants Chiara as his—for good!

#3638 TYCOON'S FORBIDDEN CINDERELLA
by Melanie Milburne

Lucien refuses to indulge in love, but delectable Audrey tests his control! Her shy innocence holds an enticing appeal. When scandal forces them together, Lucien proposes a temporary solution to their cravings—delicious surrender!

#3639 BOUND TO HER DESERT CAPTOR
Conveniently Wed!
by Michelle Conder

Certain that Regan has information on his sister's disappearance, Sheikh Jaeger steals her away to his palace. But when beautiful, defiant Regan accidentally causes a media storm, to resolve it Jaeger *must* marry her!

#3640 A MISTRESS, A SCANDAL, A RING
Ruthless Billionaire Brothers
by Angela Bissell

For Xavier, seducing stunning Jordan is a calculated risk. He's convinced their fire will soon burn out. But when their affair's exposed, there's just one option—bind Jordan to him permanently!

Get 4 FREE REWARDS!

We'll send you 2 FREE Books plus 2 FREE Mystery Gifts.

Harlequin Presents® books feature a sensational and sophisticated world of international romance where sinfully tempting heroes ignite passion.

FREE Value Over $20

YES! Please send me 2 FREE Harlequin Presents® novels and my 2 FREE gifts (gifts are worth about $10 retail). After receiving them, if I don't wish to receive any more books, I can return the shipping statement marked "cancel." If I don't cancel, I will receive 6 brand-new novels every month and be billed just $4.55 each for the regular-print edition or $5.55 each for the larger-print edition in the U.S., or $5.49 each for the regular-print edition or $5.99 each for the larger-print edition in Canada. That's a savings of at least 11% off the cover price! It's quite a bargain! Shipping and handling is just 50¢ per book in the U.S. and 75¢ per book in Canada*. I understand that accepting the 2 free books and gifts places me under no obligation to buy anything. I can always return a shipment and cancel at any time. The free books and gifts are mine to keep no matter what I decide.

Choose one: ☐ **Harlequin Presents®**
Regular-Print
(106/306 HDN GMYX)

☐ **Harlequin Presents®**
Larger-Print
(176/376 HDN GMYX)

Name (please print)

Address   Apt. #

City   State/Province   Zip/Postal Code

Mail to the **Reader Service:**
IN U.S.A.: P.O. Box 1341, Buffalo, NY 14240-8531
IN CANADA: P.O. Box 603, Fort Erie, Ontario L2A 5X3

Want to try two free books from another series! Call 1-800-873-8635 or visit www.ReaderService.com.

---

*Terms and prices subject to change without notice. Prices do not include applicable taxes. Sales tax applicable in N.Y. Canadian residents will be charged applicable taxes. Offer not valid in Quebec. This offer is limited to one order per household. Books received may not be as shown. Not valid for current subscribers to Harlequin Presents books. All orders subject to approval. Credit or debit balances in a customer's account(s) may be offset by any other outstanding balance owed by or to the customer. Please allow 4 to 6 weeks for delivery. Offer available while quantities last.

Your Privacy—The Reader Service is committed to protecting your privacy. Our Privacy Policy is available online at www.ReaderService.com or upon request from the Reader Service. We make a portion of our mailing list available to reputable third parties that offer products we believe may interest you. If you prefer that we not exchange your name with third parties, or if you wish to clarify or modify your communication preferences, please visit us at www.ReaderService.com/consumerschoice or write to us at Reader Service Preference Service, P.O. Box 9062, Buffalo, NY 14240-9062. Include your complete name and address.

HPI8

SPECIAL EXCERPT FROM

HARLEQUIN
Presents.

Sophie never challenged her arranged marriage.
Until one secret night with Renzo leaves her pregnant!
Renzo will legitimize his child—even if it means stealing
Sophie from her own wedding to make her his bride!

Read on for a sneak preview of
Caitlin Crews's *next story*
THE BRIDE'S BABY OF SHAME,
*part of the **STOLEN BRIDES** miniseries.*

"I can see you are not asleep" came a familiar voice from much too close. "It is best to stop pretending, Sophie."

It was a voice that should not have been anywhere near her, not here.

Not in Langston House where, in a few short hours, she would become the latest in a long line of unenthused countesses.

Sophie took her time turning over in her bed. And still, no matter how long she stared or blinked, she couldn't make Renzo disappear.

"What are you doing here?" she asked, her voice barely more than a whisper.

"It turns out we have more to discuss."

She didn't like the way he said that, dark and something like lethal.

And Renzo was here.

Right here, in this bedroom Sophie had been installed in as the future Countess of Langston. It was all tapestries, priceless art and frothy antique chairs that looked too fragile to sit in.

"I don't know what you mean," she said, her lips too dry and her throat not much better.

HPEXP0618

"I think you do." Renzo stood at the foot of her bed, one hand looped around one of the posts in a lazy, easy sort of grip that did absolutely nothing to calm Sophie's nerves. "I think you came to tell me something last night but let my temper scare you off. Or perhaps it would be more accurate to say you used my temper as an excuse to keep from telling me, would it not?"

Sophie found her hands covering her belly again, there beneath her comforter. Worse, Renzo's dark gaze followed the movement, as if he could see straight through the pile of soft linen to the truth.

"I would like you to leave," she told him, fighting to keep her voice calm. "I don't know what showing up here, hours before I'm meant to marry, could possibly accomplish. Or is this a punishment?"

Renzo's lips quirked into something no sane person would call a smile. He didn't move and yet he seemed to loom there, growing larger by the second and consuming all the air in the bedchamber.

He made it hard to breathe. Or see straight.

"We will get to punishments in a moment," Renzo said. His dark amber gaze raked over her, bold and harsh. His sensual mouth, the one she'd felt on every inch of her skin and woke in the night yearning for again, flattened. His gaze bored into her, so hard and deep she was sure he left marks. "Are you with child, Sophie?"

Don't miss
THE BRIDE'S BABY OF SHAME,
available July 2018.

*And the first part of the **STOLEN BRIDES** duet,*
KIDNAPPED FOR HIS ROYAL DUTY by Jane Porter.

Available now
wherever Harlequin Presents® books and ebooks are sold.

www.Harlequin.com

HARLEQUIN

Presents®

Coming next month, the first of three special *SECRET HEIRS OF BILLIONAIRES* stories by Jennie Lucas!

Hallie, Tess and Lola are all pregnant with billionaires' babies when they meet in New York City. They all have one thing in common: they haven't told any of the powerful fathers!

In *The Secret the Italian Claims*, Cristiano Moretti is furious that Hallie hid the consequences of their hot night together. He will not inflict his own childhood abandonment on his son, and demands that Hallie marry him. Soon they realize the passion between them is as powerful as ever...but when all Hallie wants is a real family, will Cristiano's seduction be enough to secure his legacy?

The Secret the Italian Claims
Available July 2018

Tess and Prince Stefano's story
The Heir the Prince Secures
Available September 2018

Lola and Rodrigo's story
The Baby the Billionaire Demands
Available November 2018

HPBPA0618

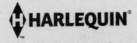